The Fallen Governess

False Rumors

Laura A. Barnes

First Printing: 2023

Laura A. Barnes

www.lauraabarnes.com

Cover Art by Laura A. Barnes

Editor: Telltail Editing

To my wonderful readers.
Thank you for your continued support!

The Fallen Governess

Chapter One

VIVIAN WESCOTT PRESSED HER hand down harder on her knee to keep it from bouncing up and down. She didn't want to draw her friends' attention to her fury, especially when they were comforting Sara Abbott and reassuring her that she wasn't at fault for their current state of looking for new employment. It was true that they had been dismissed from their positions for coming to Sara's defense when her employer thought it was appropriate to grope Sara whenever he pleased, but it wasn't the reason for her anger.

Vivian's fury lightened as she remembered Lord Baldridge's reaction when they'd made a spectacle of him in front of his peers—and at his own ball no less. Their actions had been justified for the safety of Sara's virtue. However, those who employed Vivian and her close-knit friends didn't hold the same opinion. The peers of society had deemed them unfit to educate the young minds of the future peerage, which had left them in their current predicament. Unemployed.

Vivian was well aware of how the ton turned on those who behaved with reckless actions because of the injustices handed to them. If one crossed the wrong peer in an attempt for justice, their actions set them on a path of misery. She knew firsthand how vindictive they could be. Her history with them showed proof of their coldhearted souls. Vivian held no remorse for showing the ton the true colors of Lord Baldridge. The ton hadn't ousted him, but it had left him the victim of gossip. At any function he attended, scandalous whispers of his inappropriate action would follow him wherever he led. His wife would never trust him again and would fill their homes with the oldest of servants.

Vivian held no regret for their actions other than the fate of her friends. Because of her guidance to retaliate against the ton for personal reasons, she had encouraged them to help protect Sara. Before the next morning arrived, they had found themselves dismissed without a single reference. While their fellow servants applauded their effort, and even the wives in some cases, society had deemed them troublemakers who threatened the hierarchy of their standings.

No matter the depth of their downfall, it would not undermine Vivian's determination to rise to the status of her virtue. Her parents had raised her to achieve greatness. Yes, her mother expected it in her choice of a groom and a successful marriage. However, Vivian never measured success in those terms. Greatness was in the act of her character. She had thought her choice of a groom complimented her character, but he had proven himself otherwise. At the first sign of trouble, he had abandoned her to the masses, leaving her to pick up the shattered pieces of her life and those of her family. Now it was her duty to help them rise from the ashes of their despair, along with those of her friends.

The friendships she had made over the past few months were ones she would treasure for eternity. They accepted her with open arms and offered no judgment on her past. While they'd come from humble beginnings and she'd come from wealth, it had never mattered to them. They only saw her as Vivian, not the daughter of a viscount. A person with her own thoughts and feelings. Every single one of them reminded her of her best friend, Joy.

A friendship lost but hopefully never forgotten. Vivian hoped one day the friendship would flourish again. However, for now, it remained a memory to treasure.

Vivian stared at her friends and realized it was time to deliver her news. She must convince them that this was for the best. For them to survive and make a fresh start, they needed to accept her terms. It would involve taking them out of their element and away from any nearby family. It was only for a short while until another incident amongst the ton overshadowed their demise. In the meantime, they would forge a fresh path.

She had already secured them employment in new households. It didn't leave them much time to arrive at their new positions, considering the distance they must travel. They must leave in two days to make the trip a success.

Vivian cleared her throat. "Sara, dry your eyes, my dear friend. I have promising news."

Sara sniffed into her handkerchief. "Did you find a new position?"

Vivian winked at her friends. "Indeed, I did."

Sara attempted a smile while drying off her tears. "What wonderful news."

"How fortunate for you. May we ask how you acquired this good fortune?" Grace Penrose asked with a trace of sarcasm.

Sara frowned at Grace's tone. "Yes, please tell us about your new position."

While Grace's attitude bothered Sara, Vivian only found humor in her snarl. She regarded her friends as they waited for her to describe her luck. Poor Sara. She tried to hold the wavering smile on her face, but her swift indrawn breath to keep her sorrow at bay revealed her genuine affectionate friendship.

However, Grace held skepticism about the impossibility of Vivian landing another position. With Vivian's lack of experience, her once-known status in society, and being the ringleader of Lord Baldridge's embarrassment, she would find it most difficult of all of them to find a position first.

Then there was their friend Flora Grant, who sat back, not saying a word. She only raised her eyebrow in a way that spoke of her curiosity.

Vivian leaned over and pulled out a packet of papers from her satchel. "Much to my disappointment, I was unable to secure a position in London. Perhaps England as a whole. However, the lovely country of Scotland offers me an invitation I cannot refuse. Also, I share my good fortune with all of you. I have secured a position for each of us."

"No! Absolutely not!" Flora grumbled.

Vivian knew she would meet resistance from Flora. After all, Flora had taken a position in London to escape from Scotland. She had never confided why, but from the conversations they had shared, Vivian believed it involved a disagreement with her family.

"These positions are in Edinburgh. You are from Inverness. Correct?" Vivian asked Flora.

"It does not matter. I refuse to touch foot on Scottish soil ever again." Flora's Scottish brogue slipped out with her declaration.

Grace settled her hand over Flora's to help calm her. "Perhaps we should listen to Vivian's plan."

Grace nodded at Vivian to continue with her explanation. Vivian glanced around at her friends and found their gazes focused on her as they waited for the details that might end their suffering. Vivian stood and handed a packet to each girl before sitting back down again. Each packet held the correspondence she had written in their names seeking the employment she thought best suited each friend.

She understood how she played devil's advocate, but they were out of options. They either took these positions or they would find themselves forced into unfortunate measures to secure coin. They couldn't even find positions as scullery maids, and when they attempted to gain positions at the shops in Mayfair, the shopkeepers had laughed at them. Gossip of their actions had spread to even the common folk, and no one wished to hold any association with them. This only left the horror of selling their bodies for survival. Vivian refused to have her friends lose their souls, their goodness, their virtues all because of the vindictiveness society offered them.

Vivian laid her hands over her packet. "Inside, you will find letters I have written on your behalf to gain employment. They will state the date, location, and terms of your position. Also, I included what I have learned of each of your employers. Their character, how they treat their servants, their standing in society, and every aspect of how they care for the charges you will be responsible for. I hope you will consider these opportunities because I only sought them out in your best interests. Please forgive me if I have overstepped the bounds of our friendship, but I hold great responsibility for the loss of your positions because of my selfishness."

Vivian attempted a smile in hopes to encourage her friends to consider her plan. "My actions have guaranteed us a fresh start. A new beginning. A chance to seek a new adventure. To open ourselves up to the possibilities of achieving greatness. Please take into consideration that our only means of survival is losing what we treasure most."

Grace tore into her packet with enthusiasm. "This sounds like a marvelous answer to our prayers. I am always one for a grand new adventure."

Sara bit her bottom lip, unsure if she wanted to take the risk. "Do we not hold any other options?"

Vivian gave a slight shake of her head. "I am afraid not, my dear."

Flora scoffed. "Life is full of options."

Vivian leaned back against the bench and folded her hands across her lap. "There is only one option left. Do you wish that for yourself or the others?"

Flora gritted her teeth. "You know it is not."

"What is not an option?" Sara asked.

Vivian, Flora, and Grace exchanged a look between them. Sara was the youngest of their group and the most innocent. They always took whatever means to protect her from the harsh realities of life. Her elderly grandmother had raised her in a cottage in a small village in Southern England before she passed away. Sara had never experienced the injustices of the world until Lord Baldridge.

Vivian smiled warmly at Sara. "The option is one I would not even wish upon my greatest enemy and one we must avoid at all costs. It is one where we would have to sell our bodies to survive."

Sara gasped. "Oh." Sara cast her eyes down at her lap and fumbled with the papers, bringing them up to her face to cover the blush heating her cheeks. "It cannot be our last option available."

Grace sighed. "I am afraid so."

Vivian closed her eyes at Sara's stricken expression. Soon, there came the rustling of paper as each of her friends perused the documents she had handed them. A light breeze teased the stray curls against her neck. She saw the fear in her friends' eyes, and it was the reason for keeping hers closed. She couldn't allow them to see her own fear or they would question everything she had put into motion. While Vivian was prepared to strike out to make a new beginning for herself, it also frightened her. She would leave behind everything she had once held dear.

It was necessary for her survival and for the sake of her family. Ever since her family's fall from grace, Vivian had been the only one to keep her family from destroying themselves. Her degenerate brothers still kept with their carousing, gambling, and spending foolishly. While her mother and father lived in denial, it was her younger sister, Chloe, who suffered the most. She would do anything to protect her sister from the hedonistic lifestyle her family lived. Vivian had thought at one time that she could rescue her sister when the gentleman of her dreams proposed to her. She had planned to bring Chloe into her household and offer her the secure love she deserved. However, the shame of her family's disgrace had caused Vivian's plans to diminish in the wind.

That very wind swirled around her today. As much as she wished for her friends to join her in Scotland, she must also respect their wishes if they so declined. However, she must make the journey, for it was the only way to give her sister a chance she no longer held herself. Vivian opened her eyes as silence descended on the group.

Vivian tucked a stray curl behind her ear. "Do these positions seem acceptable to you?"

Grace nodded. "Thank you, my friend. I think it is an excellent idea to leave London behind for a spell."

"I agree. Thank you, Vivian. It was most generous of you to go to these lengths for us. I do not blame you. Any of you. You hold my deepest gratitude for removing me from a situation I found uncomfortable," Sara declared.

Everyone turned to glance at Flora, curious about her answer. However, Flora stayed silent. None of them wished to rush her, but they were eager for her to take this journey with them. Flora continued to glare at Vivian for putting her in this position, which only made Vivian's smile grow wider. Once Flora growled, the rest of the girls erupted into laughter.

"I guess I am bloody well returning to Scotland."

Vivian clapped her hands. "Excellent! We shall travel to Scotland in two days. Prepare yourselves, ladies, for a new chapter in your lives. I believe this will be the first step in our chance for happiness."

Vivian rose from the bench and embraced each of her friends. Before she left, she noted their trepidation of the unknown. While she could offer them platitudes of assurances, they would only ring false. Even Vivian didn't know the outcome of their chosen paths. As they traveled along, each girl would learn if she had made the right decision. She only prayed she didn't steer them wrong and that her own path led to a favorable outcome. At this point, what else did they have to lose?

Who knew? They might find more than they had ever dreamed possible.

Chapter Two

MAXIMILIAN COURTLAND SORTED THROUGH the papers around the desk, trying to locate the one he needed. The document stipulated how he could proceed with managing his cousin's estate. His cousin had left his paperwork like he left his life, in shambles. At one time, Max used to envy his cousin for his wild and carefree attitude toward life. Seamus had appeared to hold no cares in the world. And an earl, no less.

Now he and his young wife were gone, ripped away from their two children by a fateful carriage accident. At least his cousin wasn't alone in the afterlife. Even now, Seamus probably watched him from above, laughing at him for a source of amusement.

If the children weren't his main concern, Max would laugh at the irony of the situation. However, he found himself the guardian of two young children. He must guide and nurture them so that one day, the boy could take the position his father once held. The other, he must protect and guarantee her the life she deserved.

Max raised his head when he heard a knock. "Enter."

He lowered his head again to search for the document. Max didn't need to see who interrupted him. His sister, Joy, made it her daily quest to inquire about his intentions in hiring a governess for the children. It was a daily disagreement they had held since her arrival. He put off the inevitable by not hiring one because he wanted to abide by Aileen's, his late cousin's wife, wishes. She had never hired a governess because she looked after them herself.

Even though it was expected within their standing in society to employ a governess to teach and care for the children, Aileen had held a different outlook. While Max would never admit it in polite company, he commended Seamus and Aileen's controversial parenting.

Regardless, no governess within the country would take on the position to handle the two heathens left in his care. Seamus had raised his children with a fine education, but he had also allowed them to indulge in their true Scottish traditions of riding bareback and running barefoot across the rugged landscape.

The children didn't lack manners or education. As Seamus would describe them, they were a wee bit wild. An unorthodox wildness that would meet with disapproval in society. Even at the age of four, Leah already swore worse than a Scottish warrior.

"Not at this moment, Joy. May we table this discussion for after dinner?" Max asked.

Joy held her hands on her hips. "No. This cannot wait. We must address the topic of a governess this afternoon, dear brother."

Max leaned back in the chair. "Why is it so pertinent we discuss this now?"

Joy shook her head. "You know the reason. I must return to London. My wedding is in a month's time, and Mother needs my assistance."

"Damn!" Max growled. "Forgive me, dear sister. I have stolen you from what should be your happiest moments in life to help me."

Joy sat in the chair across from the desk. "You did not steal me away. I wanted to help. This tragedy has affected me just as much as you, and I adore those children abovestairs. Even if they are a wee bit wild."

He chuckled. "Do you not mean to describe them as heathens?"

Joy's twinkling laughter help to soothe Max's stressful nerves. "Yes, they are heathens but ones we cherish."

They smiled at each other wistfully. Their smiles held the bit of sadness that could never be erased and spoke of the sorrow of their loss. The piece of their heart would forever miss their dear cousin and his wife.

Max sighed. "Very well. I will contact an agency in the morning, and we can interview the applicants. Can you stay until the end of the week?"

Joy winced. "Actually, I will make my return home tomorrow morning."

Max nodded. "Of course, I understand. The children will miss you. I will inform the servants they must assist with their care until I can hire a governess."

Joy glanced away, running her hands along her skirts. "There is no need for that either. I have taken it upon myself to hire a governess for the children, and she is due to arrive this afternoon."

Max stood, running his hands through his hair. "What? We discussed this. I am the one who needs to vet this new servant's credentials. The governess must meet the criteria for the children's education, especially Bennett. No offense, dear sister, but your intentions are only to hire someone who will coddle the children."

Joy raised her eyebrows. "What is wrong with that? They just lost their parents, for heaven's sake. Allow them some softness before you strike them with your dictatorial demands."

Max stalked over to the liquor cart and poured himself a glass of whiskey. "The children need structure and must learn discipline. Their life will change, regardless of how they feel. No longer are their days filled with their father's tomfoolery and their mother's overindulgence. They will return with me to London, where, in time, they will find their place in society after they learn the rules of etiquette and discretion. I cannot allow these children to run rampant in Hyde Park, bellowing out fierce battle cries. Bennett and Leah must learn proper decorum and the rules of our society." Determination lit Max's eyes. "No shame shall come upon them. Not a whisper of scandal has ever tainted our family, nor will it ever."

Max stared at his sister, waiting for the lecture that was sure to come since she hadn't broached the subject since her arrival. Now, with her imminent departure, she would mention it. It was sure to entail the same scathing remarks he had received from another certain young lady.

However, she was another chapter in his life that was done and over with. He refused to ponder if he had made the right decision. It was for the best of all parties involved, even if his heart declared differently. Because in the harsh reality of life, one's heart could not dictate the decisions that ruled one's life. The emotion of love held no place amongst the cruelties of life. He must abolish the feelings he held for the lady. Because any mention of her only brought forth the pain of losing her in his gut.

Joy cleared her throat. "Before I leave, I have one more request."

Max scoffed. "It would appear you have quite a list of requests today. State your thoughts before you leave. You will not rest until you do so."

Max threw back his drink and poured another one. His agitation prevented him from sitting and listening to a subject he didn't wish to discuss with another soul, even if he had shared secrets with Joy his entire life. So he would allow Joy her comments, then he would tuck them away and hope to forget them after she left.

Joy sighed. Her brother built the walls higher and higher around his heart. She didn't wish to broach the subject with him, but it was one she must address. His actions affected her as much as they affected him. His need to avoid scandal so their family's reputation remained impeccable didn't speak volumes of his character. If anything, his behavior proved him to be a shallow, callous, and coldhearted soul, not the warm and generously kind man she knew him to be.

"I love you." Joy watched Max toss back another shot of whiskey. "But you are also an arse."

Max chuckled at his sister's attempt at a Scottish accent. He quirked an eyebrow. "Arse?"

Joy pointed her finger at him. "Yes, arse. Your treatment of—"

"Do not say her name," Max bellowed.

Joy released a long, drawn-out breath. "The treatment you imparted upon your ex-betrothed fills me with shame and remorse. She was my best friend, and you trampled over her feelings as if she was some worthless street whore."

Max smirked. "Your language since arriving in Scotland has turned quite unladylike."

Joy jumped out of the chair and stalked over to her brother. She grabbed the whiskey glass out of his hand, poured herself a shot, and threw it back. Coughs racked her frame as the whiskey burned a path to her stomach.

Max poured her a glass of water. "There, there, dear sister."

She swung around. "Do not mock me, Maximilian. Your recent behavior toward her was atrocious. Why did you humiliate her in that way? She is not at fault for her father's transgressions. At one time, you adored her, doted on her, and expressed a love I had never witnessed with any other soul. I used to envy your relationship with her until I met my dear Bradley."

"We have been over this many times. My affairs are none of your concern, and how I ended my betrothal is my business alone and doesn't pertain to you. I understand your loss of a friendship. However, this remains a closed subject. Now, I have allowed you your say and I will listen to no more. When the governess arrives, you will inform her that her employment is only temporary until I can find a more suitable arrangement. Until then, dear sister, I suggest you see to your departure. I will see you at dinner."

"When did you become so cold, callous, and without emotion? Where is my brother?" Joy demanded.

"I am the same man. Just one coping with a tremendous amount of pressure. Also, trying to deal with my own loss."

Joy wrapped her arms around her brother and hugged him. "I understand how close you were to Seamus and how deeply his death has affected you. Please forgive my outburst."

Max wrapped his arms around Joy and returned her affection. "Your apologies are unnecessary when your intentions are sincere."

While the loss of his cousin affected him greatly, nothing compared to the loss of the woman he loved. She was a lady he would've fought for to the ends of the earth. However, her one act of betrayal spoke of her true intentions. The betrayal had destroyed what he had once held dear.

A commotion in the hallway distracted Max from his thoughts. A woman's soft voice rang clear. He pulled back from Joy with a questioning look and watched the swift transformation on his sister's face from happiness to guilt before she pulled out of his arms. The governess had arrived.

Max frowned. "We might as well welcome the governess and inform her of my decision."

"Max."

Max paused, waiting for his sister to finish.

Joy shrugged with a helpless expression. "There is more I need to share with you about the governess."

Max waited, but Joy only twisted her hands in front of her, opening and closing her mouth in an attempt to explain herself. He quirked an eyebrow with his impatience.

Before she offered her explanation, the butler, Bowers, opened the door. "My lord, the new governess, a Miss Vivian Wescott, has arrived. Shall I escort her to the study?"

Max gritted his teeth. "Please show Miss Wescott to the parlor. My sister shall attend her shortly." Max waited for Bowers to close the door before he growled, "Joy?"

"Hear me out," Joy pleaded and spread her palms out. "I can explain."

Max growled again. "No! Absolutely not!"

Max never gave his sister a chance to explain before he threw open the doors leading outside. He stalked toward the woods, needing to put as much distance between him and Miss Wescott as possible. Joy could give the lady her dismissal papers. He refused to lay eyes on her. Max didn't want to consider the consequences if he did.

Because they were consequences he craved but must deny himself.

Chapter Three

False Rumors

VIVIAN SAT ON THE parlor sofa with her hands folded on her lap, waiting patiently for the lord and lady to arrive. She longed to roam around the parlor and become familiarized with her new place of employment. Her mother had ingrained in her the manners of a lady, even though she no longer considered herself one. However, she would continue to act like one. If someone were to catch her trailing around the parlor and handling the trinkets, it would leave a poor impression on her new employer.

Vivian had run out of options, and she couldn't afford to lose this position, especially after convincing her friends to make a fresh start. She only prayed the Prestons hadn't heard the rumors from London of the scandal she had created with her friends and of her family's demise.

She sat up straighter when she overheard a lady's voice requesting a servant to bring them a tray of tea and biscuits. Vivian frowned. A most peculiar request since she would be a servant herself. But then meeting her new employer in the parlor was odd. The standard behavior would've been to draw her into the study to give her a list of commands and then dismiss her to begin her duties. However, the butler had welcomed her with warmth and settled her in the parlor, offering an explanation for the delay.

All of it only left Vivian to question the situation she found herself in. Were the children impossible to handle? Or was their kind behavior to take away the sting of withdrawing their offer of employment? Nonsense. If that were the case, they would've never let her step foot inside the old manor or taken her trunk upstairs.

When the door swung open, Vivian stood with the elegance of a lady, not one of a terrified servant. She gasped at the familiar face walking toward her with her hands reached out. Vivian clutched the arm of the sofa, unprepared for Joy Courtland to wrap her in a familiar hug.

Joy pulled back, gripping Vivian's arms. "It is so wonderful to see you, my friend."

Vivian opened and closed her mouth with no sound coming forth before she squeaked out, "Ahh."

Joy's laughter twinkled around them. "Sit down and I will explain."

Vivian sank onto the sofa, unsure of the situation. Her head swiveled to the door; she expected Joy's brother to walk through. When the doorway remained empty, her eyes flitted back to her friend, who sat next to her with a smile beaming across her face. No. 'Twas impossible. She was to meet with Lord and Lady Preston. Why in heaven's name did Joy greet her? Her nerves sat on edge, waiting for a thunderous roar to order her away.

A maid bustled in carrying a small tray with a teapot and two cups. Vivian relaxed at the sight. There must be a plausible reason behind her friend greeting her. Since there were only two teacups, it meant Joy's brother wouldn't join them. Why did she assume he was in Scotland? Because her heart secretly wished he was. The maid poured the tea and made a plate for each lady.

Joy waited for the maid to leave before she spoke. "You appear confused."

Vivian picked up her tea and took a sip as she tried to regain control of her scattered emotions. "Should I not be?"

Joy sighed. She detected a note of sarcasm in her friend's tone. "I will not apologize."

Vivian bit into a biscuit. "Do you ever?"

Joy shrugged. "I saw an opportunity, and I grabbed it. You cannot fault me for attempting to unite two lost souls back together again."

Vivian pinched her lips. "How does my new position relate to your brother? He made his opinion of my character quite clear the last time we spoke. Furthermore, why would you assume I would forgive him?"

"Because you love him."

"Pssh. The man is unlovable," Vivian muttered under her breath.

Joy regarded her friend and realized she might've overstepped, but she couldn't turn back now. Max and Vivian were out of options. She wished they would set their stubbornness to the side and embrace the love they held for one another. Why were they so frustrating? Since she needed to return home on the morrow, she didn't have time to ponder the dynamics of their disagreement. Max and Vivian must deal with the animosity between them and see to the children's welfare.

Perhaps, just perhaps, their love may bloom once again.

Vivian waved her hand in the air. "Explain yourself so I can be on my way."

"But you cannot. I must return home tomorrow, and Max needs your help."

Vivian scoffed. "Your brother is more than capable of dealing with any obstacle and doesn't need my assistance. I am unsure of the dilemma, but I corresponded with a Lady Preston about the governess position for two young charges. Will you please explain why she misled me?"

Joy attempted a smile but failed. Vivian's questions brought forth Joy's grief. "I am sorry for my deceit. I learned of your hardship, and I hoped this opportunity would bring about a fresh start for you. It was never my intention to bruise your ego or offer you any pity. I only wanted a chance for us to be friends again."

"Oh, my dear. You will always be my friend. No matter who you may be related to." Vivian winked.

Joy gathered Vivian's hands in hers. "Will you listen to my explanation?" Vivian nodded.

Joy squeezed Vivian's hands before beginning her sad tale. "A month ago, our cousin Seamus and his wife, Aileen, were in a deadly carriage accident. They left behind two young children, Bennett and Leah. Seamus and Aileen granted Maximilian guardianship of the children. He is required to raise them until Bennett is of age to take over the earldom and he has secured Leah a groom."

Joy brushed away a tear. "Max plans on staying in Scotland for the next month until he can settle the estate and employ a caretaker. Then he plans on returning to London with the children. He has refused to hire a nanny or governess for the children because Aileen did not believe in the strict structures that society demands. My cousin and his wife provided the children with their education but also allowed them the freedom to be children and enjoy their youth with enthusiasm."

Vivian handed Joy a handkerchief. "How tragic for your family."

Joy dried her tears before continuing. "Max does not want to go against their wishes, even though he must since he doesn't have a wife to oversee their care. He has become dependent on me over the last few weeks. However, I leave tomorrow to return home for my wedding. Since Max refused to listen to reason, I posted an ad for a governess. When your letter arrived, I could not believe my good fortune and thus where my deceit became necessary. I responded to you using my cousin's name. I thought once you arrived, the love Max holds for you would overcome him and he would plead for your forgiveness."

Vivian harrumphed. "Let me guess, your brother learned of my arrival and he stalked off into the woods."

"How did you guess?"

Vivian shook her head. "Because I have known that man half my life, and 'tis his normal reaction when he wishes to avoid a conflict. He is under the assumption that if he walks away, the problem will disappear. Only upon his return, he must deal with what scampered him away. So typical of Maximilian Courtland."

Joy unclasped their hands and stood up to pace across the room. "He is so darn stubborn."

Vivian relaxed back into the cushions. She loved Joy dearly, especially when Joy's brother agitated her. Vivian was glad she wasn't the only one bothered by Max. "Perhaps 'tis you who are so darn stubborn."

Joy stopped her pacing. "How so?"

"Because you realized the impracticality of the situation, yet you continued with the farce. Now you've placed me and your brother in positions that we cannot refuse. I cannot refuse because of the circumstances I have found myself in. And Max cannot because it would leave him with the image of being a villain. Either way, you forced us to endure each other's company for the sake of two helpless souls."

Vivian took a deep breath. "Obviously, these children need to be handled with care. Not that Max would treat them harshly, but he would insist they obey every single rule society demands, all because of his need to avoid scandal at all costs. Hence the reason behind my family's demise and his decision to end our betrothal. Oh, I do not lay blame at his feet. If he married me, it would've ruined his reputation and tarnished your good Christian family name. However, I was the fool who imagined the love we shared could overcome the whispers. Obviously, I was mistaken."

Joy stood with her hands on her hips. "Once again, I will not offer you an apology for my actions. One day, my dear friend, you will thank me."

Vivian stood. "I highly doubt so. Very well. I have no other choice because no one else will employ me. My family and my actions have guaranteed that. Shall you introduce me to the children?"

Joy clapped her hands together. "So you will stay?"

Vivian hooked her arms through Joy's as they walked out of the parlor. "Until your brother dismisses me, I will care for the children."

"Excellent. You will love them. But I must warn you, their raising has been unorthodox."

Vivian arched an eyebrow. "Am I to assume they are heathens?"

Joy laughed. "Adorable heathens."

Vivian and Joy walked along the hallway with their arms clutched together, reminiscing about when they were heathens themselves. They came to a stop when the butler stepped in front of them.

"My lady, his lordship has requested your presence in the study," Bowers stated.

"He has returned from his walk, then?" Joy asked.

"Do you not mean his sulking?" Vivian murmured.

"Yes, to both your questions, my ladies," Bowers replied before walking away.

Vivian gasped, her eyes growing wide. She thought she'd spoken low enough for the servant not to hear.

Joy giggled. "A word of warning, Bowers has a few unusual talents."

"I would say," Vivian whispered.

Joy stopped, facing her friend. "Were the rumors true?"

Vivian paused, uncomfortable with the question but also unsure which particular rumor Joy referred to. She cleared her throat. "What rumor are you inquiring about?"

"Did you really whip off Lord Baldridge's hairpiece and punch him below his stomach?"

Vivian exhaled a breath of relief, not realizing she'd held her breath. "Yes. His lordship received what he deserved."

Joy smiled. "I agree." They continued on until they reached the study. "Once we step through those doors, there is no turning back. Are you sure you wish to continue this journey?"

Vivian nodded.

Joy nodded back and knocked on the door before swinging it open. "Max …"

"Did you send her on her way? I cannot believe the position you placed me in. You do not understand the torment I have suffered from that woman's actions, nor will you ever. She is a distraction I do not need. Thank you for getting rid—" Max raised his head and was unable to finish his last thought once he noticed the source of his irritation.

Vivian curtsied. "Thank you for this opportunity, my lord."

Any other time, Vivian would've laughed at Maximilian's dumbfounded expression. However, the gentleman standing before her wasn't the man she'd fallen in love with. This man stared at her with bitterness rolling off him in waves. However, his coldness didn't catch her off guard, but the sorrow surrounding him did. Before she walked through the door, she had prepared her defense, but now she only wanted to run to him, wrap him in her arms, and soothe his troubled soul.

Maximilian Courtland left her more conflicted than ever.

Chapter Four

MAX GRIPPED THE ARMS of the chair, speechless as he gazed at his former fiancée. Her humble attire clashed with the fire blazing in her eyes. Her mockery of how she curtsied and addressed him spoke of her true nature. However, the severe plainness of her dress, lack of jewelry, and her usual flowing mahogany tresses secured in a prim and proper bun atop her head spoke of a stranger he had yet to meet. The change in her appearance, as well as her very presence, kept him shocked into silence.

While her comment had dripped with her dislike for him, her eyes spoke of an emotion they had once shared in their acquaintance. An emotion he refused to allow himself to feel toward Vivian ever again. It was the reason he had demanded his sister send her away. He couldn't afford to spend any time alone in her company. Her very presence was a weakness he'd never been able to resist. Since she accompanied his sister into the study, it meant Joy had disobeyed his demands of dismissing Vivian. Damn his meddling sister.

He noticed a few changes in Vivian his sister probably never considered. Her turquoise eyes no longer twinkled with mischief. Instead, they held a lack of gaiety. A frown marred her lovely features, replacing the dipping of her dimples with her breathtaking smile. A smile she had gifted him with enthusiasm whenever he called on her or stole a kiss from her luscious lips to hear her sighs of pleasure.

Memories he must squash. If he were to keep his sanity around Vivian, then he must remember her deceit and not allow guilt to plague him. It wasn't his fault she had found herself in the class of a servant. Nor would Max blame himself.

Max rose and walked around to the front of the desk. He leaned against it with a casual indifference he far from felt. "Joy, would you care to explain yourself?"

Joy walked over to Max and brushed a kiss across his cheek. "There is nothing to explain. Now, be a dear and do not frighten Vivian away. She is your only hope for sanity. I am off to finish packing."

Joy turned and gathered Vivian's hands in hers and whispered into her ear before leaving Max and Vivian alone in the study. To make matters worse, Joy closed the door on her way out.

Vivian bit the inside of her cheek to keep from smiling. She enjoyed Max's discomfort. She wouldn't lie to herself. Vivian suffered from a bruised heart from how Max had seemed so adamant about his dislike for her arrival. Then he had added to her suffering by ignoring her. As if she were nothing but a lowly servant, not his once betrothed who he had doted on. He acted as if his whispered words of love and their stolen kisses had never existed.

Vivian had spent the past few months convincing herself she had hardened her heart against Maximilian Courtland. But at the first sight of him, she realized she had only fooled herself. After he spoke so harshly of her character, she had never set eyes on him, and he had never given her a chance to explain herself. Instead, he had broken from the disgrace he would suffer if he continued their engagement. With her family's ruination, the ever-proper lord didn't want to have a stain tarnishing his family's reputation. And with her as his bride, he would never recover his prestigious standing in society.

"Vivian," Max gritted out between his teeth.

Vivian clasped her hands in front of her to calm the slight tremors among her fingers. "Lord Courtland."

Max raked his hands through his hair. "Max. We are well enough acquainted. There is no need for such formality."

Vivian lifted her chin. "I disagree, my lord. If I am to remain in your service, then I expect the same treatment you expect from the other servants. Nor would it make my stay among the other servants amendable if I were to address you with intimate regard."

"About that ..."

"Yes?"

Max moved to sit behind his desk. "In Joy's readiness to return home, there has been some confusion. My sister misconstrued my needs, therefore the position is no longer available."

Vivian approached the desk, noticing the disarray of papers spread across it. "Do you plan to educate and care for the children yourself?"

Max frowned. "No."

"The servants then? Do any of them hold the qualifications to teach them?"

"No."

"Then you plan to allow them to educate themselves." Vivian nodded. "That sounds like a firm plan. I wish you the best of luck, my lord."

Vivian turned and strode toward the door. She turned the knob with slow precision to give Max a chance to stop her departure. However, when her statement met silence, she realized his stubbornness would prevent him from accepting her help. She opened the door and ran into Joy and Bowers, who swiftly scattered away. Vivian paused, glancing over her shoulder to see Max quirking an eyebrow at her delay to leave.

She harrumphed and stalked along the hallway toward the entryway. Vivian came to a stop, searching for her luggage. When she didn't see it by the stairs or any servants nearby, she climbed the stairs and looked inside the bedchambers for any sign of her belongings. She stalked into the room where her trunk rested at the foot of the bed. The lid sat open, showing its emptiness.

Vivian stalked toward the wardrobe and threw open the doors. She grabbed the few dresses she'd brought with her and threw them into the empty trunk. Then she moved to the vanity and tossed the objects on top of the dresses. She wanted to scream her frustration at how Max irritated her. Instead, she set about ruining what possessions she had because she didn't know how to express her fury. He refused to listen to reason. She could help him until he found another governess.

"Stubborn, dense oaf. Still as arrogant as ever," Vivian muttered.

"Have you always held such a high opinion of me?"

Vivian stilled at Max's question. Too caught up in her tirade, she was unaware he had followed her. She turned to face him. "Only within this past year."

Max smirked. "And here I thought you still found yourself besotted with me."

Vivian rolled her eyes. "Pshh."

Vivian continued her packing, and Max bit back his smile as she muttered under her breath about his character. His presence never dissuaded her in the least. Vivian in a snit was a glorious sight to gaze upon. Throughout their betrothal, she had never shown this side of her character. She'd been the most loyal, doting fiancée a gentleman only dreamed about. That was before …

A matter best forgotten. For now, he needed to focus on the children's care. As Vivian had stated before she calmly departed the study, he was a fool not to accept her help, and he'd finally swallowed his pride.

Max pushed off from the doorway and began the task of emptying her trunk. He set her hairbrush and perfume back on the vanity. As he pulled her dresses out to place them in the wardrobe, Vivian turned with her undergarments and bumped into him. The garments fell to the floor, but he gripped Vivian's arms before she tumbled over.

"Oh." Vivian gasped.

The effect of holding Vivian in his arms startled Max. He thought he had hardened his heart toward this lady. However, the light scent of fresh lilacs reminded him of their walks in the garden. The way her body pressed against his brought forth their stolen moments when he had coaxed passionate kisses from her lips. Without thinking, he brought his hand up to brush a stray curl behind her ear. The silken strand was a whisper of a memory he longed to capture again.

Vivian's eyes widened at his familiar touch. Her heart raced at the unexpected closeness. Max's gaze clouded with the desire he once held for her. However, as soon as she murmured, "Oh," he dropped his hold and stepped away.

"My apologies." Max bent over to gather the dropped garments.

Vivian doubted her ability to remain and fulfill her obligation. When she told Joy she would, she had never imagined that the feelings she held for Maximilian still affected her so profoundly. She thought his abandonment and his refusal to believe her had snuffed out the love she held for him. However, her tattered emotions considered her pride to be foolish.

She curled her fingers into fists, fighting the need to run her fingers through his hair or stomp her feet at the unfairness of life. Either way, she must set her fanciful imagination aside and focus on her new position. The dashing lord who had broken her heart no longer held a place in her life. Except as a means for her to earn an honest living.

Max wanted to moan at the act he had almost committed. Kissing Vivian would've been a mistake he might never recover from. If he pressed his lips against her succulent ones, it would've broken the dam he had built.

On top of that temptation, he now held her chemise between his fingers. The silk was as soft as her creamy skin. He closed his eyes, and for a brief moment, he let his imagination run away with him.

He pictured Vivian standing before him wearing nothing but the sinful garment. A strap fell off her shoulder, and her hair tumbled down her back.

Her lips were plump from his devouring kisses. Her breasts strained against the fabric for release. Pebbled buds teased him with her desires.

"What is your intention, my lord?" This time it was Vivian who startled Max.

He gathered the clothing and leapt to his feet, shoving them into the wardrobe. "My intention is to beg for your assistance."

Vivian crossed her arms over her chest. "You seemed pretty adamant in your refusal by denying me the position."

Max gripped the back of his neck. "You must see how this is awkward."

"No, I do not. You are in need of a governess, and I am in need of employment," Vivian disagreed.

"You were once my betrothed," Max hissed.

"Yes. But you changed your decision and stated how unsuitable of a choice I am."

Max pinched his lips. "Nonetheless, I would greatly appreciate your help with the children until I can hire a more suitable candidate. If you can remain on as a friend of the family when Joy leaves, I will compensate you accordingly until you find a different position. I will even offer a solid reference."

"'Tis not proper. I am no longer considered a lady of standing, and I wouldn't want any scandal attached to these children because of your misguided intention. Now, I will stay on as a governess until you find a suitable replacement. In the meantime, if you will please allow me some privacy."

"I will invite my aunt for a visit to act as a chaperone."

"It is unnecessary," Vivian stressed.

"I insist."

"And I refuse."

They stared at each other. Neither of them would bend their will to accommodate the other. After a while, Max threw his hands into the air and stalked toward the door. "Fine, have it your way, *Miss Wescott*."

The air burst from Vivian's lips. She'd won this battle. As for the next one, she highly doubted it. As much as he pushed his cause, Max understood how her stay was questionable as it was, without adding more speculation to their peculiar situation. Vivian wasn't naive. The gossip from London would eventually reach the ears of the servants at this estate. And when it did, if she didn't state her status as a governess, everyone would assume she was Max's mistress. Then she would never land another position or a groom one day.

She must install herself in the household and search for a new position before she lost the ability to resist Max's disgruntled charm. A charm she found even more fascinating than the one he had bestowed on her as a doting fiancé.

Was her trip to Scotland a mistake?

Chapter Five

VIVIAN LIFTED HER HEAD at the knock on the door. Joy wore an expression that pleaded for forgiveness. "May I enter?"

Vivian waved her to come inside. "Have you come with more surprises?"

Joy sat in the chair next to Vivian. "No. I only wanted to check if you've settled and invite you to join us for dinner."

Vivian shook her head. "I must decline."

"Please," Joy pleaded.

"You and your brother are too much alike. I will dine in my room," Vivian refused.

"But in some households, the governess dines with the family," Joy argued.

Vivian smoothed away an imaginary wrinkle on her skirt. "True. However, the circumstances of my attachment to your family will make my duties difficult enough. I do not wish to add more rumors to the mill."

"Fine. If you will not submit to my wishes, will you at least make me a promise?"

Vivian arched an eyebrow. "It will depend on the promise you request."

"Will you please attend my wedding? You can travel to London with Max and the children."

Vivian's head swished back and forth in a tight jerk. "No."

Joy clasped her hands together. "Please. You are my dearest friend, and I want you to join in the festivities."

"I cannot. While I wish you nothing but happiness, it would be most improper. Nor would I wish to ruin your celebration with my attendance. You do not need the focus of your wedding to be filled with scandalous whispers but the oohs and ahhs of your peers." Vivian tried to make Joy see reason.

Joy peered at Vivian with relentless determination. "You will change your mind. I am sure of it. Would you like to meet the children?"

Vivian sighed. "I will not change my mind. And yes, I would love to meet the children."

Both ladies rose, and Joy slipped her arm through Vivian's and gave her a tour of the house. It was the standard layout of most manors. The standard dining area, parlors, library, and the overabundance of bedchambers. When they reached the nursery, Vivian winced at the banshee cry echoing along the hallway. She expected a set of tears or an argument to follow, but when they stepped through the doorway, she was unprepared to find the young girl with her foot on her brother, brandishing a sword made from a stick at his throat.

"Surrender, you Scottish traitor, before I slit your throat and steal your stag."

Vivian fought back her laughter at the scene before her. A rocking horse lay tipped over on the rug. The wild disarray of the nursery showed the children might be more than mere heathens. From what she'd gathered, their upbringing to this point had been with unabashed wildness. Then, with their parents' passing and Max and Joy indulging them, they would be a handful when she attempted to apply structure to their lives. She only hoped she could find the right balance for them to navigate the change their lives would soon entail.

The boy let out another banshee yell. "Never!"

"Then you leave me no choice." The girl raised the play sword over her head.

Joy rushed forward and pulled the toy away. "But to show Bennett some mercy."

The girl pouted. "But he raided my candy tin."

Vivian covered her mouth to hide her smile. "A most befitting punishment. One must never raid someone else's candy tin."

The boy jumped to his feet. "But Leah promised to share."

"Did you make the promise?" Vivian asked Leah.

Leah lowered her gaze and stared at the floor. "Yes," she whispered.

"Mmm," Vivian murmured. "While you made a promise and it went unfulfilled, it still does not allow one to raid another's person's possessions. I believe your argument has come to a draw."

"A fair conclusion, I would say. Do you agree, Bennett and Leah?" Joy asked.

Both children nodded at the fairness of the stranger's decision. Joy gathered each child's hand in hers and walked them over to Vivian. "Children, allow me to introduce you to your new governess. This is Miss Wescott."

Leah clutched Joy's hand tighter, while Bennett narrowed his eyes at Vivian. He showed his dislike about having someone dictate how they would spend their days. The poor dears. Their life was in an upheaval. It was clear how attached they were to Joy, and now she would leave them alone once again. Except for Maximilian. She would have to observe how he interacted with them before she voiced the children's needs to him. She only hoped he gave them the assurances they needed during this vulnerable time.

Joy's wistful smile pulled at Vivian's emotions. "Miss Wescott, this is Bennett and his sister, Leah."

Vivian smiled at the children. "An honor to make your acquaintance. I hope we get along splendidly."

"Do you like playing in the marshes?" Bennett asked.

Vivian frowned. "I cannot rightly say. I have never done so before."

"Then I do not see how we will," Bennett answered before returning to his toys.

"Do you like to play warrior princess?" Leah piped up.

Vivian lowered herself to Leah's height. "I have never had the fortune to play warrior princess. But I would love to play with you."

"All right." Leah grinned at her, and Vivian noted the girl had already lost a tooth with a new one growing in its place.

When Leah joined her brother across the room, Vivian rose. She met Joy's gaze and nodded at how she would take care of the children in her absence. Her friend moved toward the children to break the news of her departure, and Vivian left the nursery, allowing them time alone. She set off to become more familiar with the layout of the house before she started her duties in the morning. After the brief exchange with the children, she concluded she would spend the first few days learning about their personalities. Then she would complete a lesson plan.

Vivian had no intention of asking Lord Courtland if he approved. She would no longer remain on intimate terms with him. He was no longer Maximilian or Max, as she used to whisper when he stole a kiss from her lips. Going forth, she would only refer to him as Lord Courtland. Also, another habit she needed to strike from her behavior: any memory of kisses or a friendship would no longer hold any substance in their present relationship.

He was now her employer. She owed him nothing but polite indifference. No matter how dashing he looked with his disheveled appearance. Or how, when he spoke, his voice sent shivers of awareness into her soul. Their past relationship was that, their past and nothing more. She must remember how he threw her over and broke her heart.

Vivian owed Maximilian Courtland nothing but tolerance for the sake of the children. Not one show of affection.

Of any sort.

Max arrived early for dinner, hoping he could speak with Vivian before Joy joined them. He knew Vivian would arrive on time for dinner. Her punctual attendance was a trait he admired about her. However, she never came down for dinner. When he finally glanced at the table, he noticed the servants had only laid two sets of dinnerware. Max narrowed his gaze. His sister didn't plan on leaving him alone with Vivian for dinner, did she?

He tugged at his cravat, pulling it away from his throat as it choked him. When he heard the rustle of skirts drawing closer, his gaze darted to the door. Max rose, pulling his hands behind his back. He could dine alone with Vivian. There was no need to suffer from an attack of nerves. They had shared many meals.

But never alone, his thoughts taunted him.

It was simple. He would make sure a footman stayed present throughout the entire meal. Then it would leave no doubt of anything inappropriate between them.

They would spend the meal discussing the children's future and Vivian's plan to educate and care for them. Nothing more. He wouldn't allow her beauty to distract him from how he viewed their new relationship. Nor would he allow the sweet melody of her voice to soothe his troubled soul.

And for no reason whatsoever would he long to kiss her again.

Once he hardened his resolve, he glanced toward the doorway. His sister sauntered in and took her place at the table. He shoved the disappointment rolling through him to the side and refused to acknowledge how he secretly wished it was Vivian strolling into dinner.

Max continued standing, expecting Vivian to come in behind his sister. "Where is Vivian?"

Joy shook out the napkin and spread it across her lap. "She has refused to join us this evening."

"For what reason?"

"Because she believes she is below our standing to share a meal with," Joy explained, watching her brother's reaction.

However, Max refused to show his sister how much Vivian's belief affected him. He lowered himself into his seat and nodded to the footman to serve them.

While they waited for their meal, Joy smirked at him, resting her chin on her hand. He knew that look. She intended to drill him. "Why did you arrive so early for dinner?"

Max shook out his own napkin. "Because I hoped to have a word with Vivian before dinner. Since she always arrives early, I thought we could clear away any unpleasantries before the meal."

Joy laughed. "Vivian is never early for a single event. She always runs late."

Max frowned. "Nonsense. While I courted her, she was always punctual."

Joy tsked. "My brother, you are clueless where Vivian is concerned."

"How so?"

Joy shook her head. "It does not matter anymore."

"Of course it matters. Explain yourself," Max demanded.

Joy sat up straight when Bowers led the footmen carrying trays of food to the table. "I will not. You made your point quite clear regarding your feelings for Vivian, so it is unnecessary to explain her behavior from the past."

As much as he wanted to argue the point with Joy, he refused to have the servants speculate on his past relationship with Vivian. In time, they would learn of the connection. He didn't want Vivian's role in the household to become uncomfortable for her.

He waited for the footmen to serve them before he addressed Bowers. "Will you please inform Miss Wescott to join us?"

"My apologies, my lord. Miss Wescott has already eaten her meal with the children and has retired for the evening. Is there a message you wish for me to convey to her?" Bowers stood at attention, awaiting further direction.

Max silently fumed. It would appear the servants, as well as his sister, conspired against him regarding Vivian. He couldn't tell what their aim was. "Do not think I didn't notice how you placed her in the bedchamber next to mine."

"It was the most befitting room of someone of her status, my lord," Bowers responded.

"She is the children's governess and belongs in the room connected to the nursery. Not one adjoined to my bedchamber." Max attempted patience but failed miserably when he bit out his response.

Bowers defended his actions. "The chamber connected to the nursery is not befitting a lady."

Max reached for his wineglass. "Miss Wescott is no longer a lady."

"I beg to differ, and so would the other servants. Miss Wescott is every ounce a lady."

Max swung his head at his sister's giggle. Joy took immense pleasure in his disagreement with the butler. It would appear he would gain no support in the matter. "Very well. She may reside in the bedchamber this evening. However, tomorrow her belongings need to be moved to another room."

Bowers swung his gaze toward Joy in question, and she winced. "That will not be possible."

"Why ever not?" Max questioned.

"Because the children have broken the panes in the window while playing," Joy explained.

Max started cutting his meat. "Then find another bedchamber closer to the children."

Bowers grimaced. "I fear the only suitable accommodation is the bedchamber the lady occupies. The late mistress was refurbishing the other chambers, and they were never completed."

Max set down his utensils. "So let me get this straight. There are no other rooms available except for the chamber next to mine?"

Bowers nodded. "Exactly."

"Fine," Max gritted out.

Bowers bowed and left them alone to dine. With a few glances toward his sister, Max concluded that Joy was quite pleased with herself. He could call her bluff, but since he sensed a conspiracy, he knew by morning she would arrange for a few windowpanes to break and the other bedchambers to be left in a state of disrepair. When Joy wanted to accomplish a scene, she went to the extreme. It didn't matter, anyway. Vivian only held the position until he hired a more suitable candidate for the children.

"What time will you depart tomorrow?" Max inquired.

"I promised the children I would eat breakfast with them," Joy replied.

Max relaxed back in the chair. "How did they take the news?"

Joy's smile wavered on the verge of tears. "Like the warriors they are."

Max squeezed her fingers. "You will leave them in loving hands."

Joy nodded. "You understand now why I acted as I did?"

Max sighed. "Unfortunately, yes."

Chapter Six

A FTER A LENGTHY DINNER with Joy, Max retired to his cousin's study to pore over more ledgers. When the clock struck eleven, he decided to retire for the evening. He wanted to visit with Joy before she left in the morning. Also, he wished to discuss the children's schedule with Vivian before the day got underway. Max avoided looking at the door leading into Vivian's bedchamber.

Max saw to his bedtime routine since he hadn't brought his valet with him. It was only after he wrapped the robe around his body that he noticed the light glowing underneath the door. Vivian hadn't left a candle burning, had she? Right there showed proof of how irresponsible she was. Her flightiness could've burned the entire manor down.

He stalked over to the door and threw it open. Max was prepared to wake Vivian and deliver a lecture to make her ears burn. However, he came to a halt when he spotted Vivian curled up in a chair with a blanket wrapped around her shoulders, reading a book. She leaned close to the candle to capture the light.

The small flicker of the flame highlighted the touches of red in the strands of hair lying unbound around her shoulders and along her back. A section dipped to her breasts, which heaved with indignation at his coarse intrusion. He should've avoided his gaze from her breasts. It was a gentlemanly action he should've taken. However, she was a vision to behold.

The lacey garment left little to his imagination, and the swell of her breasts beckoned him for a closer look. The nightwear was one a lady would wear for her husband or her lover. Not what a governess wore.

Max gulped at the vision that was nothing compared to the dreams he had imagined of her while they were engaged. He had spent many nights fantasizing about their marital bed. Not once did he ever slake his needs with another woman during their engagement. Nor since he broke the betrothal. How could he when Vivian still held his heart?

Vivian gripped the blanket tighter around her chest. "My lord, I do not believe I gave you permission to enter my bedchamber."

Max dug his hands into the pockets of his robe to keep from reaching out and wrapping Vivian into his embrace. "I noticed the light from the candle burning and thought to—"

Vivian arched an eyebrow. "Deliver me a lecture on how irresponsible I am?"

Max bowed. "Forgive me for my inappropriate interruption."

Vivian uncurled her legs and stood up. "Contrary to what you may believe, I am not a flighty debutante who depends on a servant to cater to my every demand. I have the capability to blow out the candles before I go to sleep."

Max's treatment since she'd arrived unsettled Vivian. She knew he assumed she had betrayed him with another. But the low opinion he held of her character bothered her. While they were engaged, he had only spoken highly of her to others and treated her with respect. However, his behavior today spoke of his critical disregard for her. Another crush of boulders landed on her heart. She had thought she held his respect. Obviously, she had been mistaken.

"Again, my apologies. I did not mean to offend you."

Max noticed the hurt glistening in Vivian's gaze. He wanted to kick himself for his behavior. But it was out of his control. His emotions concerning Vivian Wescott were full of contradictions. One second, he was furious with her for betraying him. The next, he wanted to draw her into his arms, drop the blanket from her shoulders, and trace his fingers along the edge of the lace, cupping her breasts. He desired to lure her body into a mass of quivering shivers from his mere touch alone.

Vivian clutched at the blanket, her only protection between the desire coursing through her body from the heat shining in Max's gaze. She wanted to drop the blanket, throw herself into his arms, and beg for his kiss. She ran her tongue across her lips as if she could taste him. Would she savor the whiskey he drank or something more sinful?

Her gaze traveled the length of him, noting his inappropriate attire. If anyone were to come upon them, Vivian would find herself ruined to a degree where no one would ever hire her again. Max would refuse to marry her since he had already shown how her status wasn't of a quality for his bride.

However, it didn't stop her from taking in the breadth of his chest and trailing her gaze down the opening of the robe. Her fingers longed to trace every dip and curve of his muscled chest. His legs were bare. Which left her to wonder if he wore a stitch of clothing underneath. Vivian bit her lip at the vivid picture her mind conjured.

Max inwardly groaned at the swipe of Vivian's tongue across her lips. When she bit her lip while her eyes caressed him, he lost all common sense and closed the distance between them. He pulled her against him and traced his thumb across her bottom lip. Vivian gasped at his bold move, and before she voiced her objections, his tongue replaced his thumb. He traced a path back and forth across her lip, soothing it before he dipped his tongue inside and kissed Vivian with passion, surprising him.

He had craved the flavor of her since he broke their engagement. Max poured the pain of her betrayal into the kiss. Each stroke of his tongue struck out in a relentless pursuit of the agony he felt to hold her again. When Vivian met his advances with her own hunger, the kiss took on a seduction of its own. The sighs he captured melted in his mouth. Each soft moan urged him to devour her until his frustration eased.

When Max's growls vibrated in her soul, Vivian should've shoved him away, instead of melting in his arms. But with each pull of his lips making demands, Vivian slid her arms around his neck and sank her fingers into the soft layers of his midnight locks. Even though his kisses differed from the ones he'd stolen while courting her, they still brought forth the same intoxicating reaction, the kind where Vivian forgot all common sense and rejoiced in the pleasure of the intimacy they shared. She lost herself with each lick of flame that set her on fire. Vivian tightened her grip on Max's hair when he bit her bottom lip.

Vivian's tug on his hair awakened Max to how he crossed a line with her. It was never his intention to place them in this predicament. However, the style of her nightdress, the bite of her words, and the vision of her in the candlelight had urged him to throw all caution to the wind. A caution he should've heeded, but his inner wiles overruled all.

Max broke the kiss and pulled away from Vivian. "You have become more skilled with kissing since we last parted."

Vivian gasped at his assumption. The blithering sod. How dare he slander her character? She wanted to rant about her inexperience, but Max would never believe her. He had already formed his opinion and wouldn't be swayed, no matter how she defended herself or if she was innocent of his accusations. It only showed Vivian what they once shared was false. He never loved her, let alone trusted her.

Over the past few months, Vivian had learned a lot about herself. One was how swiftly she reacted when someone stirred her temper.

The fire searing from her eyes should've been Max's first warning to re-move himself from her company. However, the fragrance of Vivian as she moved closer overwhelmed his senses. So, when she raised her knee toward his cock, her assault caught him unaware. Luckily, he reacted quickly and grabbed her wrist, turning her around in his grasp. He yanked her back into his chest, and Vivian fought against his hold.

"Stay still," Max growled.

"Unhand me," Vivian hissed.

Max sighed at how uncontrollable the situation had turned, but it didn't stop him from baiting her. This side of Vivian inflamed his senses. "And even more spirited. Mmm. Which only makes me wonder in what other ways your spirit shines."

Vivian tried to rein in her temper. She heard the underlying meaning in his comment. He thought she was free with her body. That once she'd fallen from society, so had her character. She kicked back with her foot with enough force to hurt him, but she missed hitting him.

Max tightened his grip. "Where did you learn these moves, my dear?" he whispered in her ear.

Vivian gritted her teeth, refusing to rise to his bait. He already had her at a disadvantage. How he pressed himself so intimately against her backside had her fighting against the shivers of awareness coursing throughout her body. The outcome of her family's downfall had awakened Vivian to how naive she had been regarding the male species. She had witnessed enough scandalous scenes and men, who she once considered gentlemen, propositioned her to understand Max held his desire in check.

When Max curved his body around hers, a rush of warmth overtook Vivian, and when his cock pressed into her backside, her thoughts turned wicked. Every immoral fantasy an unwed female held flooded her mind. She longed for Max to gather her in his arms and carry her to his bed, where he would lay her upon the bedsheets and worship her with tender care. She didn't realize tears leaked from her eyes, trailing along her cheeks. Because she was lost in the dream of wishing for the impossible. A dream she'd lost the day he tossed her aside.

When Max dropped his hands and stepped away from her, Vivian sagged in relief. She wrapped her arms around her middle and kept from turning around and ordering him from her bedchamber. As much as she wanted to defend herself, she refused to allow him to witness her vulnerability. When she heard the soft click of the door closing, she slumped down on the bed, dragging out a ragged breath. Vivian reached up to brush her fingers across her lips and encountered the wet path of tears on her face. She squeezed her eyes shut and curled into a ball, allowing herself a moment of pity.

An action she hadn't allowed herself to express before now. It had been easy to hate Max when he broke their engagement and while she sought employment. However, now that she must rely on him for her livelihood, and in such close quarters, she hadn't realized how much she still loved him. Even as much as she hated him.

She only needed one moment more to regain her footing. Only one moment more.

Max leaned against the closed door as he tried to bring himself under control. The emotions Vivian ignited in him left him shocked at his behavior. He dragged a trembling hand down his face. Vivian's temper fueled a fresh surge of need to possess her through his veins. He had never felt a need this intense during his courtship with the lady.

No kiss they had ever shared held the potency for him to disregard his standing as a gentleman to want to possess her as a savage beast as the one they just shared. Their kisses before had been chaste, ones a gentleman sampled from his betrothed in his eagerness to make her his bride. Not the kind where he wanted to shred her nightdress from her body and ravish her without a care. He only wanted to satisfy the need consuming him and then ravish her all over again.

Because once with Vivian would never satisfy him. He wanted to possess her very soul.

It was a longing he must dispel. Not only was it inappropriate, but her betrayal would always stand between them. He could never trust her again. Also, he refused to fall into line behind every gentleman who had sampled her charms since he ended their engagement. For all he knew, she probably had fooled him during their courtship and trifled with every gentleman who so much as smiled at her.

When the familiar bitterness overcame him, he felt more stable and in control. Vivian's reaction did not differ from any light-skirts trying to claim a sense of security for herself. However, he stood by his earlier decision. She would suit her purpose until he found a more suitable replacement. In the meantime, he would keep his distance and only converse with her about the children. After he finished putting his cousin's affairs in order, he would contact a local agency and interview candidates who would suit his requirements.

Not one with soft lips he enjoyed kissing. Or one his fingers itched to caress every silken limb. Or one his body craved to press against her curves. And definitely not one whose tears made him question if he had misjudged her.

He lifted his hand as if her tears still lingered on his fingers. When the first drops splashed on his hand, Max had wanted to turn her around in his arms and apologize for his ungentlemanly behavior. Instead, he had walked away to regain his sanity. He couldn't allow her to fool him again. He had barely recovered from their broken engagement. No. He mustn't allow her any sympathy.

If it weren't for the tragic death of his cousin and his wife, Max would still be in London, getting drunk at his club every night. He hadn't coped with Vivian's betrayal in a manner he was proud of. Each night, his best mate and Joy's fiancé, Bradley, had dragged his arse home. And every morning, Joy would berate him over his behavior and urge him to seek Vivian's forgiveness. However, he would scoff at her pleas and continue with his daily routine in the same manner. Even his parents frowned over his decision and tried to persuade him to reconsider.

And throughout it all, he had never once vilified Vivian's character. He had allowed his family and peers to view her as the victim and him as the evil brute who held no sympathy for her family's disgrace.

Vivian's tears were only an act he must harden himself against. If not, then he couldn't be held accountable for his actions.

After all, tears were only a weapon used against an enemy to give one doubt.

Chapter Seven

M AX STRODE THROUGH THE manor in search of Vivian and the children. However, he couldn't find them anywhere, and the servants had made themselves scarce, an occurrence they had adopted since his sister had returned home over a week ago. It would seem the remarks he'd made about Vivian to Bowers had spread like wildfire of gossip amongst the servants. They served him cold meals, and his summons went unanswered. If it wasn't for his valet arriving after Joy left, then his clothes and bedchamber would be in disarray due to their negligence.

Meanwhile, they doted on Vivian as if she were the queen of the manor. Her twinkling laughter echoed in the hallways, and the fragrance of lilacs lingered in the air. It haunted his every waking moment. She also had managed to tame Bennett's and Leah's wildness with her calm nature—a nature she didn't extend to him after he'd kissed her so passionately on her first night.

A kiss he spent every night dreaming of. Except his dreams involved more than a mere kiss. It was only how his fantasies began. Max attempted to suppress those fantasies in the light of day. Even now, he struggled to forget them. Her cold indifference provoked him to press her for a reaction. However, she remained polite while in the company of others, which he enjoyed because at least she acknowledged him, instead of ignoring him like she wasn't aware of his presence.

As much as it annoyed him, it kept him from allowing the beast inside of him to rage over the injustice of their situation. He longed for their quiet strolls through the gardens, planning their future where she gazed upon him with adoration. The innocent smile gracing her lips as she questioned him about his day. The press of her hand on his arm as he escorted her across the ballroom floors. Vivian's whispered sighs as he stole soft kisses from her lips.

"Damn her," Max swore.

"I beg your pardon, my lord?" Bowers spoke from behind him.

Max swung around in surprise, bashing his arm on a table set that held a bouquet of lilacs in the middle of the foyer. "Must you appear out of thin air?" Max grumbled.

"I have been standing here for a while. It is you, my lord, whose thoughts have kept him from noticing others in his presence," Bowers drawled with a hint of sarcasm.

Max scowled at the insolence of the hired help. A behavior he would forbid in his household. However, his cousin had enjoyed bantering with his servants. He would dismiss the lot, but he didn't want the children to suffer from any more discord so soon after their parents' death. As much as he disliked tolerating them, the children considered the servants part of their family. Hell, some of them were. His cousin had employed members of his wife's clan and his own. Seamus had led his life differently from how Max led his. While his cousin had lived an adventurous lifestyle, Max lived a more restricted one.

One he never had trouble living until recently.

"Where is Miss Wescott?" Max barked. His train of thought made him uncomfortable.

"The *lady* has taken her charges to the park for the afternoon," Bowers informed him.

How the butler referred to Vivian wasn't lost on Max. "When do you expect their return?"

"In time for the children's dinner."

"Send Miss Wescott to the study upon her return," Max ordered.

Bowers nodded his acceptance.

Max frowned as he continued to the study. It shouldn't matter that Bowers disapproved of how he addressed Vivian. Yet it did. He settled behind the desk and was soon immersed in the estate's paperwork. However, the matter continued to linger and pricked at his conscience.

It left him wondering if he should alter his stance or stand firm with his beliefs.

Damn her.

As her friends shared the details of their new positions, Vivian watched Bennett and Leah play with the other children. She listened to them describe their new residences and their employers. She had yet to share with them the outcome of her placement. Not only would they pity her, but they would hold sympathy for her predicament. She should've asked more questions about the position. Because of her need to escape London, she had believed the correspondence she shared with Lady Preston to be sincere. It was her own darn fault for not recognizing the connection between the Prestons and Max.

Now she must spend every day living so close to him and fighting the feelings he stirred within her. Angry, yet consumed with a desire she wished to explore but mustn't.

"Damn him," Vivian muttered.

Sara gasped. "Vivian!"

Vivian glanced around to make sure the children hadn't overheard. "I apologize for my coarse language."

"Is there discord with your new employer?" Grace asked.

"That is putting it mildly," Vivian grumbled.

"A Scottish man will hold that effect on a gentile-bred English woman," Flora teased.

Vivian pinched her lips. "If only he were a Scot. I could handle a Scottish brute. Instead, he is an insufferable English prick."

Sara gasped again. "Vivian!"

However, Flora chortled with glee. "Finally, the lady has emerged into the hellion she has kept so finely repressed."

Grace sent a warning glare at Flora to quiet. "What is the trouble with your employer?"

Vivian lifted her chin. "It is Courtland."

"Is the bloke making trouble for ye?" Flora snarled.

Vivian sighed. "He is my new employer."

"How?" asked Grace.

"When I arrived for service, I discovered a past friendship had placed the advertisement for a governess. When we started corresponding, she pretended to be the mother of the children and neglected to inform me of her identity. Lord Courtland was unaware of his sister's intentions until it was too late," Vivian explained.

"What of the children's parents?" Sara asked.

"They died in a tragic carriage accident. Lord Courtland is the children's guardian. His sister, Joy, traveled to Edinburgh to help him care for the children. However, she needed to return to London to prepare for her wedding. Which left Courtland unable to secure a new governess on short notice." Vivian drew in a deep breath. "Thus leading to my fateful predicament of caring for the children until he can find a suitable replacement. Since he considers my character questionable, he has stated how he finds my attendance on the children a poor decision." Vivian cleared her throat, fighting back a fresh wave of tears.

Tears that had threatened to spill multiple times over the past week. Ever since he kissed her, her emotions had been on a turbulent wave of highs and lows. How she avoided him, except for when they passed in the halls, had been a miracle indeed. She didn't dare trust herself in his vicinity. She ranged from pouring out her frustrations at his false impression of her to throwing herself at his feet and begging for him to ruin her with his passion.

Frustrations she must resist. Because in the brief time she spent with Bennett and Leah, she had formed a bond with the children. She shared a kinship with them of sorts. They had both had their lives upended and suffered from the uncertainty of where their future might lie. She wished nothing more than to protect them from the injustices of life. While Vivian longed to hand in her resignation, she couldn't bear to part with the children. They needed her as much as she needed them.

"There, there, love." Grace wrapped her arm around Vivian, comforting her.

Vivian sniffled. "I think I still love him."

Flora cackled. "Of course you do."

"Yet I am so mad I want to scratch at his pretentious air of superiority," Vivian hissed.

Flora continued with her philosophy about Vivian's feelings. "Love and anger are but mere emotions that enable passion to flare to life. It was an inevitable outcome concerning you and Courtland."

Sara frowned at Flora. "That is enough."

Flora shrugged. "I only state what is more than obvious."

"How so?" Vivian asked.

Grace shook her head at Flora to stay silent, while Sara avoided Vivian's attention by focusing on the children. It seemed her friends held firm opinions regarding her and Lord Courtland.

"By all means, please explain yourself," Vivian bit out.

Flora smiled, pleased with drawing out Vivian's ire. "It is more than clear how you never abandoned your regard for the lord. Nor him for you."

Confusion marred Vivian's lovely features. "Have you not heard a word I have spoken? He means to replace me and leave me without a position for no other reason than a false impression he holds for an action he thought I committed."

Flora smirked. "Oh, I heard your explanation. The part you shared with us."

"I have shared everything with you," Vivian spoke with indignation.

Flora quirked an eyebrow. "Have you?"

Vivian lowered her head and smoothed away an imaginary wrinkle from her skirts. "Of course."

"Yet you have neglected to mention what Lord Courtland has done to ignite your temper," Flora pressed on.

"Vivian has explained her reasoning for her anger. He intends to dismiss her without giving her a chance to prove herself capable of the position," Grace said.

"A valid reason for her distress, if I say so myself," Sara added.

"That still does not explain why she blushes at the mere mention of Lord Courtland's name," Flora teased.

Vivian raised her head and glared at her friend. "If I blush, it is because it is a trifle warm today."

Flora scoffed. "Bollocks!"

"Flora, consider your language," Sara scolded.

Grace laughed. "Perhaps we should sympathize with our friend instead of provoking her. Especially when Lord Courtland accomplishes that task very well on his own."

Vivian stood. "Bennett! Leah! Come along, children, it is time to return home."

She had brought the children to the park today to avoid Max, hoping to gain sympathy from her friends. Instead, they set out to annoy her as much as Courtland did with his superiority. And to think she considered them her friends and had helped them to escape their hardships in England.

She turned back toward them and pasted on a smile. "I hope you have found satisfaction with your positions. My apologies for my distraction today. Shall we meet again next week?"

Sara smiled. "We shall. And please accept our apologies for speaking out of line."

Vivian nodded. "Until then."

The children ran toward Vivian, and she gathered their hands and guided them out of the park. She only half listened to their excited chatter about the fun they had with her friends' charges. Even though she desperately wanted to see her friends, she also thought Bennett and Leah might enjoy playing with other children.

Vivian was a bit perturbed by her friends' reaction to her news. Instead of offering her a shoulder to cry out her frustrations on, they had declared that she still loved Max. She had hoped they would convince her the feelings she held were normal, considering she had once been engaged to him. And since they shared an intimate proximity, it only fueled their frustrations with one another. Frustrations that, instead of inspiring dislike for the gentleman, ignited a passion she was too embarrassed to admit. Which led to her blushing at the mere mention of his name.

Why didn't she hold anger at Max for the injustices he dealt her? Why did they bring forth the heady emotions of love she wanted to share with him?

Why? Oh why?

Chapter Eight

False Rumors

MAX ATTEMPTED TO CONCENTRATE on the work sitting before him, but every noise from the passageway distracted him. What was the delay in their return? Each time Bowers passed the study, he pushed back his chair, ready to confront Vivian. If he wasn't nearby upon their return, she would flee upstairs with the children and remain out of his reach. When he didn't hear any voices, he pushed his chair back toward the desk, picked up the quill, and attempted to fix his cousins' ledgers. However, his frustration at the vexing woman kept distracting him.

Another hour passed before the sound of Vivian and the children drifted toward him. He jumped from the chair and stalked toward the foyer. Vivian helped the children off with their coats and handed them to Bowers.

"Vivian, can we go back to the park tomorrow?" Leah asked.

"Please say we can. Please, Vivian," Bennett pleaded.

"Not tomorrow, love. Perhaps next week," Vivian promised the children.

"Addressing your governess by her first name is not the proper form. Her name is Miss Wescott. Please use the correct term for her position," Courtland reprimanded the children.

Leah slipped her hand into Vivian's and hid her face in her skirts.

Vivian gritted her teeth. "Lord Courtland is correct."

Vivian had to catch herself. While her expression remained calm, she wished to snarl a reply at Courtland for his obvious set down. No matter how correct he was, it still stung her pride that he no longer viewed her as a lady but as a servant. Not to mention how his harsh tone frightened the children.

She had yet to see him interact with them except to instruct them on the matter of their behavior, etiquette, or studies. He showed them no signs of the affection or empathy they so needed. It left Vivian to wonder if she should feel relief that they had never married. She would hate any children they might've had to live a lifetime under strict control. However, her heart screamed a refusal, it wasn't the true Maximilian but a shell of the gentleman he used to be.

Leah tugged on Vivian's skirts to get her attention. Vivian lowered herself to Leah's height. "Can we go to the nursery?" Leah whispered in Vivian's ear.

"Yes, love." Vivian wrapped her arms around Leah, giving her a hug of reassurance that all was well. Vivian rose. "Bennett, please take Leah upstairs and wash your hands for dinner."

Bennett glared at Max before gathering Leah's hand in his. When Bennett suggested a game of race, Vivian didn't know if it was to annoy Max or for him to take revenge on Courtland for upsetting Leah. "The last one upstairs must offer grace at dinner." With a battle cry, he tore off, with Leah following in his wake and shrieking her delight.

Vivian attempted to hold back a giggle, but it slipped out when she noticed Courtland's disapproval. His stern expression and his fists clenched at his sides spoke of his displeasure. When he turned his dislike of the situation toward her, Vivian gasped at his turbulent expression.

"That behavior alone is the very reason you are not qualified for this position. I have been slacking in not replacing you because my sister pleaded with me to give you a chance. But now I've seen the mistake of keeping you on. Those children still behave as heathens, and instead of applying their attention to their studies, I hear you are gallivanting them around Edinburgh."

Vivian counted to ten very slowly. Her mother had taught her this trick at a young age to control her temper. She said it was never wise to let anyone know how they bested you. That if you calmed yourself before you spoke, then they would never realize how they affected you.

However, Courtland's accusations of her faults made it difficult for Vivian to stay silent. It was one matter to pass judgment on her abilities as a governess. It was another matter entirely to berate the children's behavior when they only acted as children should.

Vivian agreed the children should act properly in the company of others, out in public, or in someone's home. But within their own home, they should hold the comfort of being their true selves. Their life had severely altered, and she encouraged them to behave as if their parents were still alive. Since Courtland never attempted to engage them, Vivian felt he held no right to pass judgment on the children's actions.

Vivian held her hands out in front of her in a tight grip. "You hold the right to slay my performance since you are my *employer*. However, to announce your disapproval of the children in front of the servants is a display of boorish behavior in its own right."

Courtland gritted his teeth at Vivian's audacity. How dare she reprimand him with the servants nearby? He sensed Bowers and the other servants' disapproval. Toward him, of course, not Vivian.

Courtland wrapped his hand around Vivian's arm and dragged her toward the study. "Do not say another word," he threatened.

As he marched them away from prying ears, Vivian's skirts swished against his legs. The severe color of her walking dress looked out of sorts next to the fawn coloring of his trousers. The sight only added to his irritation. When he courted her, he had enjoyed how the pastel colors of her gowns blended with his attire. Now Vivian dressed as a widow with her dark-colored dresses. Not only did she dress without her usual flare, but she wore her luxurious hair in the strictest of buns. It should bounce against her shoulders with each deliberate step she took.

He slammed the door behind them and dropped his hold on Vivian. Courtland strode across the study and stood behind the desk, putting much-needed distance between them. When he ushered them away, he'd allowed his memories of their past to intermingle with their present situation. In remembering their past, his annoyance at how she addressed his behavior in front of the other servants vanished. All it took was touching her and the fresh smell of lilacs to forget his anger. His reaction was all the more reason to find her replacement.

Because even now he wondered if, under her drab attire, she wore the sinful chemise from her first night. Were the provocative undergarments caressing her body against the harsh material of her dress? If he rose and undid the buttons that kept her all prim and proper, would he discover the silk?

Courtland pounded his fist on the desk, frustrated with his train of thought. Vivian was a menace to his sanity. "Leave," he ordered.

Vivian stormed across the study and stopped in front of the desk, her fists landing on her hips. Her fingernails dug into her palms as she fought the urge to pound her fists on the desk. Her fury had only climbed since her outburst. He had demeaned her in front of the other servants, then dragged her away, ordering her to stay silent. Now, after his brutal treatment, he ordered her to leave.

Nay.

If she was honest, his treatment hadn't been brutal at all. It might've been abrasive the way he'd dragged her along the hallway, leaving the other servants in no doubt that Vivian would receive discipline from her harsh words. However, his touch had softened into light caresses that left Vivian speechless, and if she wasn't mistaken, it left Courtland unaware of his actions.

She lowered her gaze and took in how stiffly Courtland stood before her. Tension radiated off him in waves as he struggled with his own inner demons concerning her. She raised her gaze and met the fire burning in his, scorching her into ashes.

He still wanted her.

And he fought the need because of his ridiculous notions about the propriety he expected his family to live by. Ones that, because of her family's disgrace, she could never abide by.

Vivian took a step backward. "I must see to the children."

Courtland didn't stop Vivian from fleeing, nor did he race after her. After all, he had ordered her to leave. If she would've argued with him, he didn't know how he would've reacted. He stretched his fingers out, then clenched them again. He ached to stroke her silky skin. To caress her softness until her sighs echoed around them.

He still wanted her.

Courtland tore out of the study. "Bowers, bring around the carriage. I will take supper at my cousin's club."

Bowers stood waiting at the door with his coat and hat. "The carriage is ready, my lord."

Courtland paused. "I only just ordered it to be brought around."

Bowers held the door open. "It is my duty to anticipate your needs."

Courtland raised his eyebrow. "And what led you to believe I would need the carriage?"

"You've not had an evening out since your sister left," Bowers answered.

"And you are under the assumption I would this evening?"

Bowers nodded. "Yes, my lord. Especially after the circumstances with Lady Vivian."

"Miss Wescott," Courtland hissed.

Bowers held the carriage door open. "As you say, my lord."

Courtland climbed into the carriage and settled on the bench. His annoyance flared to life again at his servants' insolence. Not only toward the governess but with the butler too. He refused to fall for the butler's bait and discuss the situation with Vivian. Because in the end, the butler and other servants would side with Vivian.

He was the enemy in his cousin's home.

Chapter Nine

AT THE CLUB, COURTLAND settled into the armchair next to the fire and nursed his whiskey as he contemplated his circumstances. If he had any sense, he would contact the agency in the morning and have Vivian's replacement in position by lunchtime. In doing so, he would remove the source of his desires. The servants would notice the threat of losing their positions if they continued to disrespect him. Also, the children would learn discipline and structure, two factors he needed them to follow before they left for London in three weeks. They were already behind on their lessons due to Vivian's frivolity.

Vivian.

The lady was reason enough to procure a replacement. He would succumb to her charms if he didn't send her on her way soon. Living under the same roof made it more difficult to ignore the emotions she stirred to life in him. These emotions held a more powerful impact than when he had courted her in London. Their relationship had been built on compatibility, and her sweet nature had made it possible for him to love her so easily.

It compared nothing to the turbulent emotions she invoked in him now. Vivian was no longer the charming debutante but a lady who spoke her mind with a viper tongue when provoked. He desired to tame her and make her his.

"Courtland, isn't it?"

Courtland stood and stretched out a hand to Lord Lockhart, a friend of his cousin. "Yes."

"I thought it was you. Haven't seen you about since the funeral. Is your visit this evening an attempt to regain your sanity?" Lord Lockhart indicated for Courtland to sit again.

Courtland lowered himself back down against the plush leather. "A sorry attempt, but one nonetheless."

Lockhart shook his head. "A terrible shame what happened to Seamus and Aileen. How are you faring?"

Courtland threw back his drink and poured another from the bottle he had requested after dinner. "I finally have a handle on his ledgers. Now, if only I held the same success regarding the children."

"I heard your sister departed for London. Was she able to hire a governess before she left?" Lockhart inquired.

Courtland harrumphed. "The girl calls herself one, but she has yet to prove the qualifications she stated."

Lockhart poured himself a drink. "Sounds similar to a chit my mother hired for my siblings."

"Are you having trouble yourself?"

Lockhart drained his glass and poured another. "Incompetent and vexing would be the best way to describe her. Instead of keeping my siblings tamed in a respectable manner, she partakes in their hijinks. Then she has the audacity to lecture me on how I should behave toward them."

"Do you know which agency your mother hired her from? I wish to avoid using them if they refer unqualified girls for positions which require a strict structure."

"No."

Courtland drummed his fingers on the arm of the chair. "Can you inquire and send word to me tomorrow?"

Lockhart grimaced. "I cannot. My mother left for London last week."

"Did your mother not approve of the girl before she left?"

"Pshh. Another downfall of the girl. She arrived late, leaving me to vet her. My mother and I hold different opinions. While I require my siblings to fall under a rigid regime for their education, my mother believes children should be allowed to be children while they can. A sentiment she relayed to the governess in their correspondence, one the chit constantly argues after every incident of trouble," Lockhart complained.

"I can relate." Courtland sighed.

Lockhart stretched his legs out. "Even today, she carts them off to the park for the entire afternoon, ignoring the lesson plan I laid out for the day."

"My governess took the children to the park today, too."

"I guess Lord Somerville has all the luck in the governess department," Lockhart drawled.

"How so?"

"He just finished telling me how he hired an angel to take care of his daughter. He said the girl held the patience of a saint. That after a week, his daughter has emerged from her shell and skips around the house."

"A week, you say?"

"Yes."

"Does the appearance of three new governesses in Edinburgh seem suspicious? Did they arrive together? If so, we can learn which agency hired them from Lord Somerville," Courtland grilled Lockhart.

"An excellent idea." Lockhart waved over a server. "Can you please pass on my request for Lord Somerville to join our party?"

The server bowed. "Yes, my lord."

Courtland had met the gentleman only once before when visiting his cousin. Their friendship had appeared peculiar. While his cousin was a boisterous fellow, Lord Somerville was a soft-spoken gentleman who never raised his voice or acted out of character. However, Seamus had spoken highly of Somerville and mentioned how the death of his friend's wife had altered Somerville's behavior to a dramatic degree.

While he had never lost a wife, he imagined how it might shape one into another person who viewed life differently. Courtland couldn't compare his loss of Vivian to Somerville's wife. However, the heartache he suffered from dismissing her from his life had altered his opinion of love itself.

"Lockhart. Courtland," Somerville addressed them.

Lockhart pointed at the empty chair next to Courtland. "May we speak with you for a moment?"

Somerville pulled out his pocket watch and noted the time. "I have a few minutes."

"Do you care for a drink?" Courtland asked.

Somerville shook his head. "Perhaps another time. What can I do for you, gentlemen?"

Lockhart lit up a cigar. "You mentioned earlier how much your new governess has impressed you."

Somerville nodded. "Yes, she is exemplary."

Courtland sat forward. "May we inquire which agency you used to employ her?"

"No agency. I placed an ad in the *Morning Post* when I had no success in finding a suitable applicant in Scotland. Miss Abbott responded with all the pertinent qualifications in a timely manner. After a few correspondences, I decided she would be an excellent choice for my daughter," Somerville explained.

"Stalemate again," Courtland muttered.

"Stalemate?" Somerville questioned.

Courtland sighed. "It seems as if the governesses we hired arrived in Edinburgh close to the same date. We hoped you used an agency so we could discover if my sister and Lockhart's mother used the same one. We need to replace the girls we hired and believed you held information to help us."

"Sorry, gentleman. However, I can inquire with my governess if she is familiar with any ladies who need a position," Somerville offered, rising to his feet.

Courtland and Lockhart exchanged a look as if it were an option. Courtland shook his head in refusal.

"Thank you. But I will make my own inquiries." Courtland rose and shook Somerville's hand.

Somerville turned toward Lockhart and tilted his head.

"No. I will muddle through this on my own. Thank you for your offer." Lockhart nodded his appreciation.

"Very well, gentlemen. Enjoy your evening."

Courtland slumped back into the chair and accepted the drink Lockhart handed him. It appeared he must keep Vivian as the children's governess until his return to England. Once they settled in London, he would ask his mother to assist in the hiring of a new governess. In the meantime, he would avoid Vivian at all costs.

As for now, he planned to indulge in the finer spirits for the evening. It was far too early to return. He must wait until the house was abed and free of distractions.

Distraction in the form of a tempting vixen who inflamed his senses with the most provocative of images that tempted him down a path of a different indulgence.

Yes. Whiskey was much safer than a kissable governess meant for sin.

Vivian wrapped the blanket around her shoulders as she settled on the over-stuffed chair to read. After many failed attempts to fall asleep, she had finally given up and lit a candle to read her book. She tried to lose herself in the story but failed miserably. She could no more read than she could fall asleep. The same agitation from this afternoon still bothered her.

Maximilian.

When he led her into the study, she had been ready to give him a piece of her mind. However, all words had escaped her when she noted the passion simmering between them. His grip on her arm had sparked to life many tingling sensations throughout her body. And his eyes had clouded with desire when he gazed at her. At his demand for her to leave, Vivian hadn't hesitated to flee. If not, she would've made a fool of herself and thrown herself in his arms.

While Vivian and the children ate dinner, Bowers had interrupted and informed her how Lord Courtland decided to spend the evening at the club. She didn't understand why he told her of Max's plan, other than to reassure her of a pleasant evening. It didn't go unnoticed how the servants treated Max in her favor as if she were the mistress of the home. Not him the master. Their display this afternoon only showed him in a less favorable acceptance, and they offered Vivian their sympathy.

Now she sat befuddled by her emotions. She refused to leave the children in their state of grievance. Nor would she allow Max to bully her into abandoning her duties just because his nose was out of joint. If he would've allowed her to defend herself this afternoon, he would've learned how she had viewed Bennett and Leah in their element this past week to give her a better understanding of how to teach them. All children absorbed learning in different ways, and these children were curious creatures who required an unstructured learning environment for their needs. Also, she must address his involvement with the children. Children only thrived when treated with love from their parents—or guardians in Bennett's and Leah's case.

As she tossed and turned in bed, Vivian's imagination had conjured many possibilities for Max's delay in returning home. She kept coming to the same conclusion that he had found a lady to spend his evening with. She wasn't a fool to believe he had remained celibate after he broke off their betrothal. Max was a very viral gentleman who would seek his pleasure since he no longer held any obligation to remain faithful. Vivian rubbed her hand over her heart at that piercing thought.

Vivian shook her head to clear away her heartbreaking thoughts. It was no use dwelling on Max's whereabouts when his actions were no longer any of her concern. She had three weeks to help the children become accustomed to the changes in their lives. Then she would travel with them to London and help them settle in Max's home. After she helped them settle, she would visit her family for a spell, then embark on a new position. It was time for her to move forward. Hopefully, once she returned, the gossip would've died down, and she could find a position that kept her close to her sister.

She blew out the candle, ready to sleep so she could implement her plan in the morning. However, before she crawled into bed, a loud crash came from Max's bedchamber. Vivian rushed to the door. She almost opened it before she realized it would be a mistake. The last time Max saw her in her nightdress, it had reminded her how much she still loved him. His fiery caress across her body, mixed with his delicious kisses, had brought forth how much she desired him. It was the very reason she had avoided him all week.

Another loud crash echoed throughout the silent house. Vivian pressed her ear to the panel and heard Max curse. When she heard glass break, Vivian rushed into the room to quiet Max's fumbles before he woke the other servants or the children.

Max swayed on his feet and squinted at Vivian. "Ahh, there she is. The infamous governess who consumes my every thought."

Vivian frowned at his comment. Max was sloshed. He had stripped his suit coat off and thrown it over a lamp. Which explained the broken glass. Now he hopped around, trying to pull off a boot. If she didn't get him seated, who knew what other damage he would incur in his drunken attempt to disrobe.

She moved to guide Max into a chair. "Sit while I clean up your mess."

Max spread out in the chair. "At your command, my lady."

Vivian rolled her eyes in exasperation at his behavior. She bent down and picked up the broken glass, setting it on the hearth. Then she used the fireplace brush to sweep up any slivers of glass she might've missed. When she turned around, Max was sleeping. She moved to his side and began the work of removing his boots. An act she had performed many times when her brothers had come home too drunk to take care of themselves.

After she divested him of his boots, she stood back with her hands on her hips. Vivian debated whether to undo his cravat and unbutton his shirt or to throw a blanket over him and let him sleep off his overindulgence. The part of her that was irritated with him urged her not to even cover him and just return to her bedchamber. However, the part of her that wished to care for him prompted her to make him comfortable for the night.

She stepped in between his legs and tugged on his cravat, loosening it until it came undone. Vivian lifted her hair and hung it around her neck. Her fingers trembled while she undid the buttons on his shirt. Her knuckles scraped across his neck as she worked to free each button from its hole. His warmth seeped into her hands, spreading throughout her body. She gulped at the sight of his broad chest that rippled with muscles as his shirt draped open.

Once she thought Max would rest comfortably, she backed away. Or so she attempted to.

However, what she neglected to notice as she unbuttoned Max's shirt was how he had awakened. Now he had his hands wrapped around the ends of the cravat and pulled her back toward him. Vivian landed on his chest, her hands lying flat against the muscles she had only just admired. She raised her gaze to meet Max's smirky expression.

A shiver of the unknown caused her to tremble.

Chapter Ten

False Rumors

"EVEN THIS IS BENEATH you, sweet Vivian. I never thought you would stoop to blackmail. But I must admit how brilliant of you to trap me into marriage because you fear I will dismiss you," Max drawled.

If Vivian thought Max's inebriation would keep him from his cruelty, then she'd been mistaken. He spoke the brutality of his accusation with crisp precision. She shoved against his chest, but he only held on tighter. She wanted to smack the smirk off his face. And to think she had considered offering him comfort. Of course, he would misconstrue her caring intentions and twist them into vile slander of her character.

Vivian pounded on his chest. "You insufferable brute. Let me go at once."

Max's fingertips grazed along her back. "Why would I do that? When I can seek pleasure from your trap."

Vivian tried pulling away again, but Max kept a firm hold on the cravat, leaving her bound in his grasp. As much as she wanted to bash his head and knock some sense into him, the fire licking across her back at his soft caress befuddled her thoughts. His hand drifted lower, caressing her buttocks. Max tugged at her nightdress, pulling it up her legs until his fingers met her bare flesh. It knocked her into an inferno, the flames blazing her common sense to ashes. His touch left her speechless, unable to resist him.

In the brief time he was passed out, Max never in his wildest dreams imagined such a tempting display would await him when he came to. The same silk chemise caressed Vivian's lovely body. The thin straps sliding off her shoulders only made her more of an enticing vision to behold. Her hair had come unbound and hung about her shoulders in disarray as she had undressed him. His cravat slipped through his fingers as he drove his hands through her hair and drew her lips down to his for a kiss.

The intoxicating flavor of honey coated her tongue when he slid his tongue past her lips. He groaned as her lips softened under his and her moans vibrated against their kiss. Soon, Vivian wrapped her arms around his neck and slid her fingers into his hair, tugging him closer.

Max rolled them over in the chair, where he hovered over her, not once pulling his mouth away. The kiss grew more passionate with each fiery lick of his tongue against hers. Vivian's soft breasts pressed against him and her nipples hardened against his chest. He slid a hand away from her hair and along her neck. His fingers traced the lace filling out her breasts before dipping under the fabric and curving under her breast. The globe fit his hand with perfection. Max brushed his thumb across the stiff peak, back and forth. Vivian's body shuddered at his touch.

When he pinched the bud, the hitch of her breath turned into a deep sigh so profound it ricocheted through his body, turning his cock to stone. His sense of how inappropriate his behavior had kept him from tearing the flimsy garment off Vivian's body and ravishing her throughout the night. However, it wasn't enough for him to pull his lips away from hers. He moved lower to take the hardened bud between his lips and sucked with the greed of a thirsty man seeking his salvation on the essence of Vivian alone.

"Maximilian," Vivian moaned.

Vivian moaning Max's name should've been the incentive to demand her release. However, each time his tongue stroked her flesh, her body begged for more, overriding any rational thought. His harsh accusations faded into mindless chatter as her body came alive once again. Vivian's eyes traced his kiss from one breast to the other through her eyelids weighed down with heady desire, capturing her in Max's trap. A trap he had accused her of, but one he carried out.

When his palms slid her chemise higher, exposing her core, Vivian shivered. She must put a stop to his attention before they ventured into a territory neither of them wished to travel to. His rejection still stung to a point where Vivian was unsure if she was capable of ever forgiving him for throwing her over. Yet her body rejoiced at his mere touch.

The position she found herself in meant a life of servitude. She would never experience the touch of a man unless by force. Why should she hold back from allowing her wildest fantasies to come to life? Especially from the gentleman who used to hold her heart in the palm of his hand. She could harden her heart against his slanderous words and prepare for another round of his rejections, as long as he never stopped with his bold caresses and fiery kisses.

Vivian pressed his head against her breast as an ache consumed her soul. She didn't have a clue what feelings overtook her body; she only knew Max eased the ache with his rapt attention. She wiggled underneath him, searching for relief. However, when Max drove his hips in between her thighs, the ache only intensified. Her fingers dug into his arms as she rocked against him, seeking the unknown.

Vivian came alive underneath him. Her breathy sighs echoed around him. The softness of her thighs beckoned him to explore higher. His palm brushed across her curls before diving into her wetness. He raised his head when Vivian's sigh turned into a breathy moan. He slid a finger across her dewy clit and dragged it down to slide inside her pussy. Vivian arched her neck, her breasts pushed forward. He lowered his head again to draw a bud between his teeth as his finger built a rhythm inside her, causing her to press down on his hand each time he drew out.

He ached to drop between her thighs and drink from the well of her core. To draw his tongue across her folds while her wetness filled his mouth each time he sent her over the edge.

But he'd already crossed a line he might never recover from. To risk his chance of losing Vivian, he must pull back before insanity dragged him under and never allowed him to resurface again.

He had always wondered how Vivian would respond to his lovemaking. Her kisses had always been so sweet, and he hungered to explore more between them. However, he had held back until they spoke their wedding vows. When the day never happened, it never stopped the vivid dreams of Vivian in his bed.

His earlier thought made him pause. To risk his chance? Had he changed his mind about Vivian's role in his life? Did his heart hold the ability to forgive her for her past indiscretions? Or would he always wonder whose bed she shared beside his?

"Max." Vivian's throaty whisper shook him from his thoughts.

Her head thrashed against the cushions with the need consuming her body. He had pushed her to the edge. With a few more strokes, she would fall. But would he catch her or let her crash into oblivion? She had turned into a wild creature he created by stroking her desires to the surface. While he kept his desires repressed, he wanted nothing more than to send her flying. To lose himself in her passion and hold his arms out to catch her when she recovered.

Max slid another finger inside as her pussy tightened, enticing him in deeper. Her juices dripped onto his palm with each stroke, drawing out her need. He bent over and ravished her mouth, stealing one kiss after another as Vivian exploded around them. She clung to him as her body shook.

Max lightened the kiss, softly brushing his lips across hers until her trembling body settled against his. Max wasn't a fool to think she'd fallen asleep. No. The longer he held her, the more the light of their actions sank into her conscious, causing her to stiffen against him. She didn't push him away but held herself still, unsure of his reaction to their desire.

He sighed, pulling away from her and rising to his feet. Max dragged the cravat through his hands, still too much of a coward to acknowledge his actions. Even when he watched her out of the corner of his eye as she lowered her chemise to her knees and pulled the silk over her breasts, sliding the straps over her shoulders. Once she stopped moving, he finally glanced at her to find her sitting straight with her hands folded in her lap. Even sitting all prim and proper with her hair in wild abandonment and her lips plump from his kisses, she was a beauty like no other.

However, Vivian's astonished look of embarrassment and shame had the effect of someone throwing water in his face. He quickly sobered as the consequences of his seduction lay before him. Vivian's orgasm had rocked him to his core.

He realized then that there was no other lady for him than Vivian Wescott.

However, his actions were of a reprobate who took advantage of a lady unable to defend herself. Max's shame settled with unexplainable doom over his conscience.

Vivian sat frozen in the armchair over her wanton actions. As she put herself to rights, she noticed Max's reaction. Regret rolled off him in waves. While her body still tingled from the rush of their desires, he only wanted her to leave. However, Vivian wondered if her legs were steady enough to allow her to return to her bedchamber with an ounce of dignity. Dignity she no longer held, because she allowed her desires to overrule common sense.

Vivian pushed herself to her feet and fled to her bedchamber. She slammed the door and turned the key to keep herself away from Max. Then she ran to the other door and locked it, too. She stood in the middle of the bedchamber, lost as to what she should do next.

She must pack and prepare for Max's dismissal tomorrow morning. It was the only outcome awaiting her. The way she'd allowed him to touch her only confirmed his accusations of her scandalous behavior. When he first slandered her character, she'd been an innocent maiden and had continued to be. Until this evening in his bedchamber.

However, Max wouldn't view her as innocent. She covered her ears, trying not to imagine the cruel words he would throw at her. Especially after she had acted the hussy at his bold touch. She sank to the floor and fought back tears. While Max had set her soul on fire tonight, he had also killed the hatred she held for him.

Now she feared she couldn't survive without him.

Max followed Vivian, but she slammed the door in his face before he could voice his apologies for taking advantage of her. He feared she would flee before he explained his behavior. He tried the door, but she'd locked it. Max tore out of his bedchamber and approached the door from the hallway. But she'd locked this door, too. How could he prevent her departure without revealing his reasons? Besides pounding on the door and threatening to kick it down, he only held one other option. Bowers.

Instead of returning to his bedchamber to make himself presentable, he rushed to the butler's quarters and pounded on Bowers's door. At least, Bowers's room was a distance away from the other servants. Not that it mattered because his butler kept the gossip vine flourishing with fresh material daily. With him as the principal source of entertainment. However, he couldn't risk Vivian slipping away unnoticed before he spoke with her.

Bowers opened the door with Max in mid-swing from announcing his arrival. "How can I assist you, my lord?"

Max frowned. Did Bowers sleep in his attire? "I apologize if I have awakened you."

"Nonsense, Lord Courtland. I am but a humble servant available at your every demand," Bowers drawled.

Max noticed the sarcasm dripping from the servant's tone but ignored it. "If Miss Wescott requests assistance to depart, I need you to delay her departure until I speak with her."

Bowers took in Lord Courtland's disheveled appearance and the smell of a distillery with each word he spoke. "May I inquire why Lady Vivian would make such a request?"

Once again, Bowers made it clear he favored Vivian over him. Could he trust the servant to make good on his demand? Or would he aid Vivian's escape if she requested? He held no other option but to place his trust in the servant.

"Nothing that concerns you. I only ask you to fulfill my request for the lady's protection. Will you?"

Bowers nodded. "I will as long as it concerns Lady Vivian's safety."

Max nodded and strode away without another word to Bowers. Bowers held the ability to make Max doubt himself with just the arch of an eyebrow. While he should be the one to intimidate the servant, he couldn't risk the butler's defiance. In fact, he should work on gaining the servant's respect if he hoped to win Vivian over.

Once he realized he wanted her no matter the circumstance, a sense of peace overwhelmed him, and hope blossomed for their future.

Now to convince Vivian of his true intentions.

Chapter Eleven

THE BANSHEE HOLLERING STARTED as a slow drone invading his sleep and transformed into a roar the closer it drew to his bedchamber. Max rolled toward the window and noticed the dark sky. Why were the children playing at this hour? Because they lacked discipline, that was why. Another fault to add to Vivian's list of failures. It seemed to be an unending list, the more he noted. Even her ...

"Oh, my goodness! Vivian," Max muttered, springing out of bed.

He wobbled on his feet at the pounding in his head. Max groaned as he threw on a robe and stalked to the door. He threw it open and roared, "What is the meaning of all this commotion?"

The children dropped their play swords, backing away in fear. Max cringed at their actions. He didn't mean to frighten them, but they must learn how inappropriate their behavior was. There were consequences for playing during bedtime. However, yelling at the children wasn't the best course to take. Especially as he noticed how Bennett pulled Leah behind him to protect her. As he should have. However, Max wasn't the enemy, only the guardian who expected them to behave in the manner of their standings.

Max took a deep breath to approach the children with patience. He glanced at Vivian's door and hoped they hadn't wakened her. How she slept through the disruption was a wonder to begin with. He must return the children to their beds so he could sleep off the rest of his headache before he faced Vivian. When had his life become so complicated?

"Can you explain to me why you are playing instead of getting a full night's rest?"

Bennett glared at Max and tilted his chin in defiance. "Because it is not our bedtime."

Max narrowed his gaze. "I beg to differ, young man." He pointed to the window. "The darkness paints a different picture."

Bennett pointed his sword at the same window. "'Tis dark because it storms."

Max moved toward the window. When he stared outside, he saw the clouds move with rapid speed across the sky. A light haze hovered underneath them, attempting to peek out, but the fierce winds kept them hidden. A bolt of lightning lit across the sky.

"Shouldn't you be eating your breakfast and working on your studies? Where is Miss Wescott?" Max asked over his shoulder, listening to the rain pelt the windows.

"Breakfast was hours ago," Bennett told him.

"Miss Wescott already said her goodbyes." Leah sniffled behind Bennett.

Max jerked around and barked, "Her goodbyes?"

His tone caused Leah to cry. Bennett sent another glare toward Max, wrapped his arm around Leah's tiny frame, and led her away, not offering Max any more of an explanation, only trying to protect his sister from Max's wrath. However, the boy couldn't be more mistaken. Max wasn't furious but panicked. Had he lost his chance to apologize to Vivian?

Max felt torn between wanting to reassure the children he wasn't upset with them and needing to learn Vivian's whereabouts. His need to find Vivian won out. He would talk to the children later.

Max knocked on Vivian's door, but she didn't answer him. He opened the door and stepped inside. The soft scent of lilacs met him, wrapping him in memories of her soft skin against his. The farther he stepped into the bedchamber, the more he realized she'd left. None of her belongings lay spread out amongst the tables or the bed. He moved to the wardrobe and knew before he opened the doors that he would find it empty. Still, he tried, wishing her clothes still hung inside and her bag rested on the bottom shelf. But not a single item filled the piece of furniture.

"Bowers!" Max roared.

He didn't care what the servants thought of his unruly behavior. He was a man desperate for knowledge of the lady he had compromised with his ungentlemanly behavior. A lady he carried gut-wrenching feelings for longer than he cared to admit and had thrown over because of his pride. Where had his pride gotten him, except to live a miserable existence? Once again, he had allowed his superior attitude to leave Vivian without security.

"You bellowed, my lord?" Bowers addressed Max from the doorway.

"Miss Wescott? Where did she go? Did she take the carriage? You agreed to keep her from leaving," Max demanded.

"And I have followed your orders. Lady Vivian has waited with patience in the study since daybreak for you to arise from your drunken debacle."

Max growled. "I was not drunk."

Bowers gave a slight bow. "As you say, my lord."

The butler turned and left Max fuming, displaying his insolence by not waiting for Max to dismiss him. Max followed him, but when he reached the corridor, Bowers had disappeared. He continued on, stomping down the stairs on his way to the study. Each servant he passed stopped their chores and stared at him in shock. Then they swiftly averted their gazes and scurried away. He found Bowers standing by the door to his study, waiting for him.

The butler then had the audacity to raise his eyebrows as if he disapproved. "My lord, perhaps you wish to prepare yourself before talking with Lady Vivian?"

Max stormed past Bowers, irritated with how everyone in the household behaved toward him. It didn't help how his head ached with more pressure from when the children had awakened him. "Return her luggage to her room and close the door. I wish for privacy while talking with *Miss Wescott*," Max snarled.

Bowers mumbled, "English prick," before he closed the door.

Max bristled at the comment but remained calm before confronting Vivian. He stalked over to Vivian, who was sitting all prim and proper in the chair before the desk, with her hands folded in her lap, staring straight ahead. She hadn't flinched once she heard his approach. He moved to stand in front of her to gain her attention, but she never flicked her gaze at him once.

He cleared his throat. "Vivian?"

Vivian closed her eyes for a brief second before she turned her gaze upon him. "*Lord Courtland*, if you can please refrain from using my Christian name, it will make this ordeal much smoother to deal with."

"I will do no such thing, *Vivian*."

"Do you not mean *Miss Wescott*?" Vivian gritted out between her teeth.

Max sighed. He deserved her venom. This morning hadn't proceeded with how he'd planned before he fell asleep early this morning. He must find a way into her good graces if he wanted forgiveness for his scandalous behavior.

He lowered himself to the level of the chair to get her attention. "I do not wish to argue this morning. Can we please call a truce?"

With Max standing, Vivian had kept her gaze focused just beyond his head to stare at the storm raging outdoors. But when he bent to her level, it drew her focus away to stare at his supreme form. She had willed herself not to become distracted by his devastating body dressed in immaculate style. Max decked out in full attire had always weakened Vivian's resistance to his arrogance. After their intimacy the night before, she held no willpower in resisting Max. Also, his soft tone wore away at her defenses.

After she left his bedchamber, Vivian had stared at the shadows on the ceiling until she fell into a restless slumber. She'd berated her behavior and tried to find any excuse for why she'd succumbed to the touch of his kisses. But every reason twisted into a jumble of rubbish. After she awakened, she had packed her belongings and found Bowers, requesting his help to leave. However, the butler had convinced her to break the news of her departure to the children. By the time she finished, the storm was raging with the same fury coursing through Vivian.

Since Bowers refused to endanger the other servants to aid in her escape, he had directed her to the study to await Max. The butler would help secure her a carriage ride into town when the weather cleared. Vivian had agreed and waited for Max. However, morning soon turned into the luncheon hour, and still Max never arrived.

Until now.

Vivian lowered her gaze to stare at Max's boots. However, his bare feet peeked out from underneath his robe. Robe? Her eyes widened as her gaze rose, taking in his bare legs to the belt tied around his stomach. She paused there, gulping. Her thoughts turned to what lay beneath. Warmth flooded Vivian as her gaze continued higher to see his chest on display from where the robe gaped open. Vivian wasn't too naive to understand Max wore not a stitch of clothing underneath.

Her mouth watered at the sight. It would only take one tug and his robe would separate before her very eyes, displaying every delicious inch of him. Every improper, immoral thought flashed before Vivian's vision. Oh my! She needed air. Not only to breathe but to cool her scandalous imagination.

Then, as swiftly as her wanton thoughts consumed her, the reality of the situation hit her like a ton of bricks.

She sat alone with an unmarried gentleman who clothed himself in a robe, wearing nothing underneath. With her position as a governess, she no longer considered herself a lady. However, the ordeal was most inappropriate. It tarnished her reputation amongst the other servants. Rumor would spread before she even held a chance of finding another employer. At this rate, she would need to flee to the Continent to gain employment. She'd barely escaped the rumors in England to find a position in Scotland. Now even Scotland would remain out of her reach. What was Maximilian's agenda to address her in this attire?

Vivian jumped out of the chair, keeping them separated. "Where are your clothes?"

Max frowned at how Vivian's voice cracked. He peered down at himself to take in his clothing. Damn! In his rush to discipline the children and discover Vivian's whereabouts, he had neglected to dress before coming downstairs. Bowers's comment finally rang clear. The butler had attempted to warn him but not to the degree required of him. The universe had set out to sabotage his sanity.

Max rose and secured the robe tight around him. Not wanting to shock Vivian, he moved behind the taller chair at the desk, blocking him from her view. His action was absurd since she'd already taken in the sight of him wearing next to nothing. Now he understood why the servants reacted as they did. Oh damn! The servants.

He had hoped to reassure Vivian he wouldn't step out of line again and that she had nothing to worry over. He now gave the servants room to gossip about his relationship with Vivian.

"I can explain," Max began.

Vivian turned her back to him. "There is no need."

Max ran his hands along Vivian's arms, and she jumped in surprise. "Please give me a chance."

A tingling sensation coursed through Vivian at Max's nearness, sending flickers of shocks throughout her body with his touch. If he dared to kiss her, Vivian would be powerless to resist. She must stand firm in her resistance. It was her only option for survival. "I imagine you have done enough damage that any explanation would only fall on false ears."

Vivian spoke the truth, but he at least wanted to try. He must if he ever hoped to redeem his behavior from the past few months. Especially since she'd arrived in Scotland. He turned her around to face him. When she continued to avoid his gaze, he tipped her chin to force her to look at him.

"Please, Viv," Max whispered

Whenever Max whispered his nickname for her, it was the start of her demise. He only had to flash his charming smile and her knees weakened and she'd agree to whatever he wished of her.

She wanted to stomp her feet at her unfortunate luck and her lack of willpower. Why couldn't she stay angry with this man? Why did he always leave her wanting more?

"You have ruined me."

Max hung his head in shame. Whether she referred to last night or the circumstances they found themselves in now, it didn't matter because he had on both counts. "It was never my intention."

Vivian stepped away from Max, rubbing her hands up and down her arms. She believed Max spoke the truth. However, it didn't solve their issues.

"Will you offer me passage back home to my family? I must secure a new position. Also, will you write a letter of reference in my regard? I understand you believe I do not deserve one, but I offer my gratitude if you would, nonetheless."

Max leaned against a bookcase, watching Vivian move farther away from him. She thought to put distance from them, as if it would keep the sexual tension simmering between them at bay. He fought to keep his smile hidden at her naive intentions. Vivian had much to learn, and he would find much pleasure in teaching her. If she thought to run away, she was mistaken. He had no intention of losing her again.

"I am afraid I must deny your requests, *Vivian*," Max taunted.

Vivian growled. "May I ask why, *Lord Courtland?*"

Max crossed his arms in front of his chest. "Because you have yet to fulfill your obligations under my employment. I believe your contract stated you would see to a schedule for the children's education and implement the schedule with a daily routine."

"But my employment was only temporary until you found a more suitable replacement. Were those not your exact terms?" Vivian argued.

"Yes, they were. However, I have yet to find your replacement. Until I do so, you are required to stay. Now that we have settled that issue, shall we discuss your appearance in my bedchamber? It was inappropriate behavior on your part. Can I expect your assurance you will not cross those improper lines again while under my employment?"

Max couldn't help but goad Vivian. Her temper slowly boiled while he refused her demands and provoked her by reminding her of their scandalous interlude. He enjoyed watching her fume. She was delightfully arousing when in a snit. A trait she had never once displayed during their betrothal.

"My behavior?" Vivian sputtered.

Max pushed himself off the bookcase and strolled to her side. He couldn't help but notice the slight hitch in her breathing or the way her eyes darkened the closer he drew to her. He pressed his lips to her ear and whispered, "While I found the encounter pleasurable and one I would enjoy partaking in again, we must do so behind closed doors. Not ones open where anyone might observe our passionate exchange. You understand how my position warrants so, Vivian dear?"

Vivian reacted before allowing herself a chance to respond to Max with a calm demeanor. The audacity of him to suggest there would ever be a repeat of the previous evening! She stomped on his bare foot. Granted, her footwear was soft and would do him no everlasting harm. However, it didn't stop her from grinding her shoe with a force strong enough to make him pull back and hop away.

She opened her mouth with a rebuke to set him in place. However, nothing was uttered past her lips when his robe came loose and she received a full view of his godly form. No longer would her imagination wonder about a single inch of him. Max put the statue of *David* to shame with his perfection. Her gaze remained fixated on his glorious muscles that rippled on their own accord.

Max cleared his throat, and Vivian raised her gaze to see a satisfied smirk covering his face. She growled at her mortification and pushed past him, knocking her elbow across his face as she attempted to shield her eyes.

She never stopped until she reached her bedchamber, where she found her luggage sitting on the bed. What started as a simple escape had turned into an ordeal she couldn't possibly walk away from unscathed.

Vivian collapsed onto the bed. She needed to rethink how to force Max's hand into dismissing her with no rumors attached to her name. Spending time alone with her employer while he only wore a robe didn't help her cause any. She refused to believe his taunting words meant he wanted more from her. Other than an affair, that was.

While Vivian pondered her next course of action, Max set his plan into motion.

Chapter Twelve

V IVIAN AND THE CHILDREN sat at the dining room table, waiting for Max to arrive for dinner. She hadn't sought his permission for Bennett and Leah to dine as adults. Nor did she join them because she wished to enjoy Max's company. She wanted her position in the household known as only a servant. Her role was to intertwine the children's and Max's lives with as little fuss as possible. She wanted to deliver a message to Max and the servants about the severity of her role and how no nefarious activities existed between her and Max.

Leah giggled at Bennett as he attempted to hang the spoon from his nose. Vivian fought back a smile. The young lad reminded Vivian of her brothers and the mischief they had attempted in their youth.

Her smile turned bittersweet as her thoughts turned toward home. It was ridiculous to feel homesick when her own family didn't even miss her. Well, everyone but her sister. Chloe was the only reason Vivian had remained after her exchange with Max this morning. She wanted her sister to enjoy a season before her family fell even more into ruination.

Vivian heard footsteps coming along the corridor and patted the table for Bennett to put down the spoon. She then motioned for the children to sit like serene angels as she'd instructed them before they came downstairs. These children were her priority before she could provide a better life for her sister. Their future hung in the balance. Would they continue to enjoy the life their parents had set out for them, or would it become a litany of proper decorum set out by their guardian? Vivian believed they could compromise on a middle ground, and it was her goal to achieve the outcome.

"Now, remember to be on your best behavior this evening," Vivian reminded the children.

Max strolled into the dining room with a book underneath his arm and came to a halt when he spotted them sitting around the table. Vivian sat up straighter, prepared for his rebuke. However, he nodded at them and took his seat. She relaxed her shoulders at his acceptance but remained on guard because she didn't quite trust how he would proceed.

"Lord Bennett. Lady Leah. Miss Wescott. It is a pleasure to dine with you this evening." Max nodded at each one of them as he addressed them by name.

"Courtland," Bennett replied like a mature gentleman.

"Our pleasure, Cousin Max." Leah smiled at Max.

Vivian wanted to smirk and stick her tongue out at Max. And he thought the children were nothing but heathens. Max arched his eyebrow at Vivian's smirk but never commented. He signaled for the footman to serve them. Vivian shook out the napkin by her plate and laid it across her lap.

Vivian had confided her plan to Bowers, and they had devised a menu suitable for the children to enjoy and to appease Max's appetite. A light but hearty meal. When the servants served the first course, the children followed her example, mimicking her every move. Her heart swelled with pride at their attempt to act with proper decorum.

Max waited until the footman served the second course before he attempted a conversation with his guests this evening. While it thrilled him that

Vivian had joined him for dinner, he was unsure of her intentions. She had avoided him throughout the day at every attempt he made to speak with her. How one lady could be so elusive was beyond him. It didn't help with the servants aiding her in staying out of his reach. However, as the afternoon wore on, he had allowed Vivian privacy and bid his time until the house went to sleep for the night. Then she would have nowhere to hide. Not even the sanctuary of her bedchamber. He'd make sure of that.

Max sliced through the chicken on his plate. "How were the children's lessons today?"

Vivian nodded at Bennett to answer the question.

Bennett laid down his eating utensils. "I spent the morning working on my arithmetic, and this afternoon, Lady Vivian read to us from a book about Greek mythology."

Leah bounced on her chair with excitement. "There were gods and goddesses. And mythical creatures."

Vivian smiled at Leah's pronunciation of the word mythical. She struggled, but her enthusiasm more than made up for the error.

Max frowned at the children's explanation. He wanted to reprimand the children for answering when he had directed his question toward Vivian. Also, he didn't recall Greek mythology being a subject in their curriculum. His complaints continued with how Bennett referred to Vivian. He had been very specific about how the children should address her. However, the children were no more inclined to call her Miss Wescott than the servants. Another matter to discuss with Vivian later this evening.

"It sounds like you had a fulfilling day." Max took a bite of the chicken.

"Then we walked to the pond, where we had afternoon tea," Leah gushed.

In her excitement at having Max's attention, she accidentally knocked over her drink. Once the milk started flowing in Max's direction, Leah's mouth trembled. Vivian rushed around the table, attempting to stop the accident from escalating. However, the milk spilled over the edge onto Max's lap. The cool liquid splashed against his trousers, staining the fawn material.

Max jumped out of his chair with a growl. Leah burst into tears, crying hysterically.

Their simple dinner turned swiftly to chaos. Bennett attempted to comfort his sister while glaring at Max. The footmen scrambled to clear the mess on the table. And throughout the entire ordeal, Max fought to keep his arousal at bay. Because Vivian's reaction had been to blot her napkin across the front of his breeches. His cock hardened under her care. It didn't matter that the dining room was filled with servants and children. The only thought consuming him was Vivian peeling away his trousers to finish her ministrations.

Max grabbed her wrist to stop her movements. "I suggest you withdraw your hand before you cause a scandal neither one of us can recover from." He then pressed her hand against his hardness to emphasize his point before he dropped it. Max moved behind his chair to hide his excited state before anyone else noticed.

Vivian gasped, mortified by her actions. Never mind how Max made it worse by making her aware of his arousal. She had made an innocent attempt to help him, but somewhere along the line, it had turned scandalous. She felt her face growing warm, and her gaze darted around to see if anyone witnessed her attention toward Max. To her relief, luck rested on her side. Servants darted around the table to clean the mess, and Bennett wrapped his sister in a hug.

The evening had started out promising and now ended on a horrible note. She had hoped to engage Max with the children. They would only survive their ordeal if they forged a bond with one another.

Vivian moved toward the children and knelt to their level. She whispered to them, "I am very proud of you children this evening. Do not distress, love." Vivian rubbed her hand along Leah's back. "'Twas only an accident. Now, run upstairs and I will send dessert up to the nursery. After your baths, I will read to you."

Leah wrapped her arms around Vivian's neck and clung to her. "Will you come with us?"

Vivian returned her hug before rising. "I must speak with Lord Courtland first, and then I will be along."

"English prick," Bennett muttered, pulling his sister after him.

Vivian thought the same. She turned toward Max to find he had resumed his seat with a fresh plate before him. He pointed at Vivian to return to her seat so they could proceed with dinner. She had no other choice if she wished for him to view the children in a different light. She was their only advocate for what awaited them in the future.

Vivian returned to her seat, setting the napkin back on her lap. With careful precision, she sliced the chicken and ate with delicate bites, waiting for Max to lecture her. While he had always held a carefree attitude when he courted her, underneath, she knew about his need for control. His current situation was a disorganized disaster of diabolical ends. Since her stay in Scotland, she had witnessed different facets of Max's character she hadn't seen before. Which left her unsure about how to proceed.

He stayed silent through the rest of the meal, watching Vivian squirm and dart looks at him between her lashes. During this time, he thought about how to approach their dilemma without sending Vivian into hiding. It seemed the only way to secure her compliance was to agree to her demands. Or at least make it appear he was agreeable.

Max stood after the servants cleared the dishes. "Thank you for joining me for dinner, Miss Westcott. If you would please join me in the library, we may continue our discussion from this morning." He waved his hand along the length of his body. "As you can see, I am fully clothed. Also, I will allow the door to stand open so there is no question of the safety of your virtue."

English prick, indeed. Bennett had the right of Max's character this evening. No matter how much she wished to refuse his request, he left her with no other choice. Earlier this morning, she had allowed her emotions to govern her hasty decision to leave. But once she came to her senses, she had decided to fulfill her contract until Max found a more suitable replacement.

She realized she held the power to push Max to hire someone qualified to his specifications sooner if she irritated him to a small degree. Like, for instance, reading to the children about Greek mythology and spending the afternoon walking to the pond. She already had plans to annoy him tomorrow. However, she must proceed with subtle changes and not all at once.

Vivian rose. "Lead the way."

In any other circumstances, Max would've held out his arm to escort Vivian or at the very least walked behind her. However, the divide between their classes had him walking in front of her. He might've pressed her status since she had arrived in his employment, but an uneasiness settled over him as she trailed behind him like a servant. Max missed how her fingers curled around his arm when they paraded around like a couple. He missed the sway of her skirts against his trousers and how her breasts innocently pressed against his arm with their closeness.

Once Vivian settled in an armchair, Max moved to pour them each a glass of wine. While he'd sworn not to imbibe with spirits while Vivian remained under his employment, he made the excuse to himself of how ineffective the potency of the wine was. It was too mild for him to act out of character.

Vivian accepted the glass and took a sip. She set it on the table next to her and folded her hands in her lap. "Thank you."

Silence hung heavy in the air between them. Each time they glanced at each other, their gazes darted away. Even though the door stood open for anyone to see them acting with proper decorum, the atmosphere simmered with a sizzling crackle. Vivian had never felt more aware of Max than she did now.

Max pulled out his timepiece and noted the time. "I would like to discuss our evening before you retire for bed."

"Perhaps we should wait until tomorrow morning. I need to see to the children's bedtime."

"I will not keep you long. Would you care to explain the children's presence at the dinner table this evening?"

Vivian tilted her chin. "This afternoon, they shared with me about how they used to eat meals with their parents. I thought it was a perfect opportunity for you to spend time with them. I have noted since my arrival how you never visit with them."

Max leaned his arm on the fireplace mantel. "And why would I?"

"Because you are their guardian," Vivian explained.

"And as their guardian, I know what is best for them. Your position as their governess is to follow the guidelines I set out for them."

Vivian narrowed her gaze. "Will you treat your own children in the same manner you do Bennett and Leah?"

Max straightened to his full height. The tone of Vivian's question voiced her disapproval. However, he stood firm in his beliefs. Children, while they were a parent's pride, must also refrain from certain activities until they reached a certain age.

"Of course."

Vivian shook her head in disbelief. And to think she had planned to marry this man and bear him children. She never thought his rejection would hold such relief. She could honestly reflect on that sentiment now because of her annoyance with him. How he held these viewpoints was beyond her. Max's parents had never held this opinion that she could recall. She held fond memories of running through their hallways with Joy when they were younger. His parents would laugh and encourage their games of amusement. She even remembered Max acting like Bennett when he was younger. Was his newfound responsibility the cause for his prickly demeanor? Or was there more to his change of attitude?

Vivian stood and fisted her hands behind her back. "Then I must thank you for breaking our betrothal. For I would have been miserable in a marriage of such existence. And I pray for any children you may have one day."

The brunt of Vivian's words settled like venom in Max's gut, urging him to lash out. "As I would suffer the same, especially when I would always wonder who my wife cuckold me with."

Vivian gasped. For him to speak so poorly of her character hurt with a deep profoundness. However, she pushed the pain to the side. "Well then, you will be in constant worry, no matter who your wife is. You would drive any sane woman into another man's arms."

Max stalked over to Vivian and pulled her against his body. "I didn't hear you complaining last night," he hissed into her ear.

Vivian attempted to shake off his hold, but Max only gripped her tighter. Her body betrayed her by softening against him. As much as she should pull away, she couldn't resist the joy of being held in his arms. If she turned her head, their lips would brush against each other.

She glanced toward the door to make sure nobody lingered outside. When she heard footsteps, common sense returned, and she shoved away from Max. "You did not give me much of a chance to. Did you, Lord Courtland? An innocent maiden trapped under your hand while you took advantage of her. I was powerless under your prowess."

"Powerless." Max scoffed. "Innocent, I hardly doubt. In fact, your response only proved how free you are with your body. If I were to inquire, I'm positive it is the reason for your dismissal from your last position."

Vivian paled at the mention of how she had lost her previous position. It was clear Max didn't have a clue about the incident involving Lord Baldridge. If so, he wouldn't have hesitated to throw her behavior at her feet. She only hoped he never learned of the situation. She didn't want to risk her friends' current positions because she couldn't hold her temper in check again. It seemed to be a recurring habit of hers of late.

Bowers interrupted them. "Please excuse me. Lady Vivian, the children are ready for bed and await their story."

"Thank you," Vivian said before rushing out of the library.

"Vivian, we are far from finished with this conversation!" Max shouted, stalking after her.

Bowers stepped into his path. "My lord, while I commend you on keeping the doors to the library open while speaking with Lady Vivian, the volume of your discussion and what you discussed did not bode well for the lady's reputation."

Max's only response was to scowl at the butler. He didn't take kindly to a servant reprimanding his behavior toward Vivian like a parent would scold a child. He pushed past Bowers and continued toward the study, where he would spend the remainder of the evening savoring his cousin's whiskey. Max may have sworn off the spirits while Vivian resided under the same roof, but the maddening emotions coursing through him urged him to lick his wounds.

The whiskey understood his predicament and sympathized with him.

Chapter Thirteen

False Rumors

V IVIAN LEANED AGAINST THE door, breathing a sigh of relief at avoiding Max. She had spent the past hour consoling Leah and calming Bennett from exacting revenge against Max. Well, as much as a young lad could exact his revenge. Vivian prayed he refrained from putting frogs in Max's bed or filling his tea with water from the pond tomorrow.

Vivian grimaced at Bennett's list of retaliations. Not only from the acts alone but from how Max would react to them. Her attempt to forge a bond between the children and Max had ended in disaster. To top it off, his vulgar attack on her character had set her temper aflame. She wished to take her own retaliation but realized how futile the outcome would be. Max had his mind set. He considered her a wanton hussy, and her behavior since she had arrived in Scotland only reinforced his opinion.

She pushed off from the panel and moved to the wardrobe to change into her nightclothes. After hanging her dress, she stood in her chemise, staring at her reflection in the mirror. She didn't recognize herself. The carefreeness of her youth had faded into a woman who fought for her survival. Frilly dresses made of silk no longer adorned her body. Now she clothed herself in the garments of a governess. Plain day dresses made from cotton that was easy to clean. Instead of a lighthearted smile gracing her face, a frown settled in its place. Her hair hung in disarray after corralling the children into bed.

If she was still a lady, her maid would adorn her hair in the latest style with ribbons or jewels. Instead of longing to crawl under the quilt, she would be attending a ball or soiree. And the man who infuriated beyond reason would be her escort. Now, she stared daggers at the closed door separating them. She wanted to yank the door open and deliver Max a set down of her own. While the other part of her wanted him to open the door and seduce her with his touch and his wicked smile. How did one man provoke such a variety of reactions from her?

Exhausted from the trying day, Vivian crawled between the sheets instead of changing into her nightdress. She loosened the ribbons and settled against the pillows, hoping to fall asleep before Max came abovestairs. If she stayed awake, it would only send her thoughts down a path that would ruin what reputation she had remaining. Max would gloat that he'd been correct in his opinion of her character. Why she had never corrected him when he broke off the betrothal was beyond her.

She'd tried to convince herself that he deserved better than to be associated with her family and their downfall. However, she failed when her heart refused otherwise. No matter how many tears she cried and the promises she swore to herself, she couldn't move on from the heartache of losing Max.

Vivian closed her eyes and drifted to sleep. As with every night, her last thoughts were of Max proclaiming his love.

The simple dream escalated into a nightmare, with her turning around in circles, searching for Max. But she only saw a vast blackness closing in, with his snarling laughter echoing all around her.

Vivian dragged herself awake, sitting up with her breaths coming out in ragged gasps. She clutched at her chest and drew in a deep breath to calm herself. Once she settled, she leaned back against the pillows. A slight movement to her side caused her to still. She didn't need to glance in his direction to know Max had entered the bedchamber after she fell asleep.

"Now, what troubles you to have your sleep filled with a nightmare?" Max drawled.

"'Twas not a nightmare, but an annoying monster pestering me in my sleep," Vivian answered, drawing the sheet over her chest.

"No need to cover yourself in my regard."

"With the comments you make toward my character, it is very much needed."

Max tipped the whiskey bottle to his lips and drank a long swallow. "On the contrary, I have decided to view your character and its captivating attributes in a new light. A flattering one at that."

"You are snockered again," Vivian accused.

Max set the bottle on the ground and sat forward in the chair. "Actually, I'm quite sober. I've refrained from indulging. I intended to drown my troubles in my cousin's spirits. But after the first drink, it only brought up memories of sharing a drink with Seamus, bringing forth many nostalgic sentiments."

Vivian wanted to comfort Max with an affectionate gesture when his tone turned melancholy. Since the chair sat in the dark corner, she couldn't see his expression. She stayed silent, unsure what to say. No matter how she responded to him, he would twist her words to suit his benefit.

"I've reached the conclusion that if I want these children to behave with any amount of proper decorum when I take them to London, I must heed your advice. But for me to make this concession, you must agree to my terms," Max stated.

"What terms might those be?" Vivian asked.

"I will make an attempt with the children by taking afternoon tea with them. Then, once we finish, we can take a stroll either through the gardens or across the grounds. Perhaps even take a ride."

"That seems perfectly acceptable," Vivian agreed.

Max's deep laugh should've warned Vivian, but in her excitement about how he agreed to spend time with Bennett and Leah, she ignored it.

Max smirked. "Not so quick, my dear. There is more to this proposition than my spending time with the children. There is the aspect regarding your role."

Vivian gulped. "And that would be?"

"You will dine with me every evening. Then once we finish dinner, we will retire to the library for a nightcap."

Vivian narrowed her gaze as a sense of uneasiness settled over her. "I do not see how spending time together is constructive to the children's development."

"It isn't."

"Then I do not understand what your motives are."

Max rose and moved into the moonlight's path. A wicked smile spread across his face. "No motives. You can chalk it up to my desire to enjoy a lady's company while I am stranded in Scotland."

Vivian pinched her lips. "What sort of company?"

His annoyingly sexy laughter echoed around them. "Why, Miss Wescott, what kind of gentleman do you take me for?"

"The question is more, what kind of lady do you take me for?" Vivian snarled.

Max moved to sit on the edge of the bed and brushed Vivian's hair behind her ear. He lowered his head to whisper in her ear. "A lady who sets my senses aflame with a need so profound that I wish to kiss her senseless until she agrees to my terms and then continue until I have captivated her with my desires, where she only wants to succumb to my need to make her mine."

Vivian didn't know if it was Max's affectionate gesture or the provocative words he whispered in her ear that left her unable to resist his seduction. Perhaps it was the countless days of loneliness that caused her to soften under his touch. Or maybe her heart rejoiced at the attention he paid her. Whatever the reason, it urged her to turn her head so his lips would brush across her cheek.

Where they continued until they landed against her own. Soft kisses urged her mouth to open under his. Bold strokes of his tongue coaxed her capitulation to his desires. The lingering flavor of whiskey coated her taste buds, making her hunger to get drunk from his kisses. Vivian floated back against the pillows, and Max followed, lying on his side next to her. She turned to press herself against him, her body craving for any contact from him.

It wasn't Max's intention to seduce Vivian. He'd only whispered those words to provoke a reaction from her. She had his mind muddled with continuous thoughts of her, and he wanted her to suffer the same. While he had felt sentimental drinking his cousin's whiskey, it wasn't the reason for his distraction or the need not to imbibe. He had snuck into Vivian's bedchamber for a chance to be near her, unaware, without harsh words spoken between them. However, the longer he sat watching her sleep, the more he realized the pull she held over him. He wanted her in his bed. Perhaps if he made love to her, he could detach himself from the fascination he felt for her. He didn't remember her consuming his thoughts while they were engaged, not as she did now.

When Vivian sat up in bed and the straps of her chemise slid off her shoulders, it had provoked him to whisper scandalous thoughts in her ear. He never imagined she would respond to him so willingly. Or with such eagerness.

Max wrapped his arm around Vivian's waist and brought her flush against him. He had discarded his suit coat, vest, and cravat before invading her privacy. It allowed him to enjoy how her hardened nipples brushed across the thin material of his shirt. After capturing her moans between their kisses, he trailed a path along her neck to the ribbon holding her chemise in place. With deliberate care, he pulled it loose from the hooks until nothing remained to keep him from her heaving bosom. With each indrawn breath she took, the garment drew apart and gifted him with a tease that drove him into a madness he'd never experienced before.

Her delicate skin glowed in the firelight. His hand hovered over to pull the fabric aside, while his conscience drilled into him how he could never turn back if he proceeded. He would be a rake of the highest order by taking advantage of Vivian's weaknesses. A scandal would ensue if someone discovered them.

However, when he raised his gaze to Vivian's, he found her staring at him with a need so profound. Her ocean-filled eyes swirled with untamed desire, leaving him shaken to his core. It wasn't Vivian who would succumb to his desires, but he who would succumb to hers. He had always thought he held the upper hand, but it was Vivian who held the power.

He was but a slave to her devotion, and this knowledge unsettled him.

Vivian watched the torrent of emotions flash in Maximilian's eyes. The desire transitioned from unleashed need to the enormity of the situation if he continued his seduction. She watched him struggle and was powerless to help him decide. Vivian had decided as soon as Max claimed her lips. She wanted him with an urgency no proper miss should ever feel unless it was for her husband.

She wasn't a fool to believe Max would be overcome with love after she gave herself to him. However, the need to belong to him, if only for this precious night, ruled her actions. While the harsh realities of life stripped her bare, they couldn't steal away whatever memories she created along the way. And the memory of Max making love to her was one she wanted to treasure for all of eternity.

Call her actions scandalous, but she no longer cared. She laid her hand over his and helped to pull the chemise from her breasts. She held no clue how her urging would diminish Max's control. His reaction left her spellbound and shaken. Not from fear but from the desire rippling off him in waves, leaving her eager for his destruction.

With a single pull, Max tore Vivian's chemise from her body, leaving her bare to his intense gaze. His eyes roamed every inch of her, indulging in the magnificent sight before him. A blush spread from her cheeks and trailed along every delectable inch of her. The brush of pink only added to her beauty. His gaze lingered on her breasts, and her buds begged for his mouth to suck upon them. However, he kept his hands to himself, allowing his sight to indulge in the wickedness of his actions.

His gaze moved along to the curve of her hips, where he would grip as he plowed into her. His tongue swiped out to lick his lips with eager anticipation when he focused on her curls and the delights hidden beneath. Max hummed his approval before roaming the length of her legs. His cock hardened at the image of them wrapped around him while he slayed their passion. This night wouldn't be enough for him to tame his cravings for this woman. He would need countless evenings to fulfill every desire he held for Vivian.

Max rolled off the bed, not giving Vivian any warning about where his thoughts had transpired. Humiliation flooded her senses at her bold actions. She'd thrown herself at Max, proving everything he'd said about her to be correct. Tears flooded her eyes, and she barely kept them at bay. She reached for the quilt to draw over her naked limbs.

Rejection clawed at her heart once again.

Chapter Fourteen

M AX PULLED HIS SHIRT over his head, oblivious to Vivian's distress. When he focused his gaze back on her, he saw the quilt drawn against her body. Her lips quivered, and tears sat on the verge of her eyelashes, ready to spill. He frowned at what had brought on her change of behavior. Then he realized that when he rose from the bed, he'd led her to believe he only toyed with her. Which was far from the truth.

"Vivian." Once he had her attention, he tugged at the placket of his breeches to show her he was far from finished with her. "Pull the quilt away from your body," Max demanded.

Vivian's breath hitched at Max's forceful growl. He peeled his trousers off, standing before her every inch a man aroused. His hardness jutted out from his body, hard and beating with a pulse of its own. Vivian's eyes widened when his fingers wrapped around his cock and slid up the length. Obviously, she had misunderstood why he rose from the bed.

"Now!" Max ordered.

She complied, and once again, Max stroked the flames of her desire when he admired her body. He didn't even have to touch her, only caress her with his eyes and a sense of empowerment settled over her. The emotion gave her the bravery to extend her hand for him to join her.

Max shook his head. "All in due time, my dear. For now, I wish to memorize the vision before me. Ingrain into my thoughts how amazing you look spread out waiting for me. Thoughts of you like this always made my cock hard, but seeing you lying in the flesh, bare for my admiration, makes my ache swell with a need so powerful to make you mine."

The passion blazing from Max's eyes inflamed Vivian's senses and made her act as boldly as him. She wanted him to act on his needs and only thought to provoke him, not expecting him to unleash his desires on her so profoundly that it left her a trembling mess. But her naivety on the limit of the male's ability to stay in control pushed Max past the breaking point.

Her breasts felt heavy, and she ached for a relief she was unfamiliar with. She slid her hands along her sides and under her breasts, cupping them, while her thumbs brushed across her nipples. Max hissed, and the blaze in his eyes burned brighter. It was all the encouragement she needed to continue. Pinching her nipples between her finger and thumb, she tugged at them. Vivian closed her eyes at the sensation coursing through her body. While it helped to ease the ache consuming her, it also added another level of throbbing she knew only Max could ease.

Since she now understood how the power of touch inflamed her senses with her own body, she assumed the same reaction if she were to touch Max in the same way. While keeping one hand on her breast, she reached out with the other to wrap her fingers around Max's cock. Her thumb brushed across the tip, gathering his wetness and rubbing it in small circles. It was the ultimate act to push Max to unleash his passion on her soul.

Max had tried to rein his need in, instead of claiming Vivian as his. It was the reason he hadn't touched her yet. His body shook with the uncontrollable desire to strip away Vivian's vulnerability and turn her into the wanton temptress of his dreams. Already she proved herself capable of possessing the qualities with her brazen act of touching herself and then him. Her actions drew him further under her spell. A spell he wanted to dominate her senses with, instead she left him spellbound and unleashed.

He grabbed her wrist and drew her hand away from his cock. With a wicked grin, he settled her hand on her curls and guided her fingers to sink into her slick wetness. Vivian attempted to jerk her hand away, but Max held firm. He slid their fingers over her clit and along her folds. She tried to pull away again.

"What is the matter, sweet Vivian? I thought you wanted to play?" Max drawled.

Vivian's hand paused, and indecision crossed her features. He meant to taunt her with the dare, never expecting her to continue. However, she relaxed her fingers once again and helped to guide them toward her pleasure. Her body arched off the bed when he guided them to slide inside her pussy.

"Maximilian," Vivian moaned.

Her moan undid what remained of his control. He grabbed her wrist again and pinned it at her side while he crawled onto the bed and settled between her thighs. He dropped his hold and spread her open wider. Her dewy wetness beckoned him to fulfill his need. Vivian's hand wandered back and slid into her folds, teasing him with her abandonment.

"No!" he growled.

She wouldn't find pleasure with her own hands any longer. He would be the only one to draw out her satisfied moans. He nudged her hand away with his head before he struck his tongue out to lick along her folds. Max wrapped his hands around her thighs and pulled her into his mouth. He inhaled her arousal with each swipe of his tongue. Soft, slow strokes to savor her essence soon turned into the frenzied lashings of his unquenchable craving. One taste didn't satisfy him. And each one after only added to his demise. Each drop of her wetness heightened his need to possess her soul.

Vivian thrashed her head back and forth on the pillow as Max attacked her senses. Every act he committed was indecent and immoral. Entirely improper. Beyond wicked and wanton. Yet willfully fulfilling. With each stroke of his tongue, Vivian soared to an unknown destination. Max sent her body rippling in waves when he slid his fingers inside her. Each pull in and out built an unbearable ache she never thought she'd survive. But when his tongue teased her clit with gentle flicks, the ache eased and she relaxed. Then he continued the pressure by adding another finger inside her, increasing his strokes with rapid succession and sending her spiraling over the edge.

"Maximilian." Vivian groaned in blissful agony as she shook all around him.

Licking his lips, Max raised his head to see the rapture on her face. Vivian tilted her head back with her eyes closed. She held her mouth slightly open as her chest rose with each rapid breath she drew in. Max placed his tongue on her clit and pressed down before flicking back and forth. Vivian's eyes opened, staring at Max in wonderment as his tongue swirled around and around. When his teeth scraped across the hardened bud, her teeth clamped down on her bottom lip, a groan escaping. A fresh wave of juices slid across his tongue.

His Vivian was a responsive goddess that he must claim for his own. Now! His desire to possess her pressed him to enter her with a forceful push. He slid his cock into her pussy to the hilt. Her body recoiled from the force, and Vivian whimpered from his harsh treatment. He stilled and looked down at her in confusion. The pleasure swirling in Vivian's gaze disappeared, then filled with shock.

She'd been a virgin.

Max leaned over, resting his elbows above her shoulders. His fingers glided through her hair. "Forgive me, my love," he murmured. "Take a deep breath and try to relax."

At Max's urgings, Vivian followed his directions. The brutal invasion of his arousal had caught her unaware. His continued murmuring helped her to relax and allowed her body to adapt to Max stretching her. Soon a warmth overtook her at the pressure spreading her apart. She moved underneath him, and another wave of pleasure coursed through her. Still, Max never moved a muscle.

Vivian's surprise didn't overwhelm her to where she was unaware of Max's shock that she had been a virgin. She knew he believed the lies from his peers concerning her virtue. She would dwell on the betrayal later. For now, she wanted Max to finish making her a woman.

"Make love to me, Maximillian," Vivian whispered, brushing her fingers through his hair.

Max closed his eyes at her husky tone and the touch of her fingers stroking his hair and running along his neck to his back. It would be so easy to give in to the temptation she requested. To move between her legs to seek his gratification. To bring her to the pinnacle height of satisfaction. To make her his. However, his damn conscience demanded that he withdraw from her.

He opened his eyes, unprepared for the desire still blazing in Vivian's eyes. "I thought …" Max shook his head and attempted again. "I never should have …"

There were no words to help soothe his brutal treatment. He should've taken her with the slow patience a gentleman would bestow on an innocent. Not roughly and so caught up with passion that he treated her like a mistress. Regret plagued him, but her pussy clenching around his cock wiped away any coherent thought.

Vivian pressed her finger against his lips. "Shh."

Vivian understood Max enough to know that reality would soon return and he would compartmentalize their act of passion and the assumptions he'd made. If she didn't draw them back into their desires at this moment, she would lose this stolen memory forever. She didn't want his false platitudes or broken promises or any charity he would offer. She only wanted him as a man to her woman. Two souls intertwined for this brief period of time. She wanted the bliss he would gift her if he would only move past his regret. And she knew only one way to achieve her wish.

She pressed her lips against his neck and trailed a path to his chest while grinding her hips against his. Max's body tensed, and she smiled. So she continued her assault on his senses. She placed soft kisses toward his nipple, where she glided her tongue around to draw it between her lips. Softly sucking on the bud, she rotated her hips again, enjoying the thrilling sensation of pleasure coursing through her. When Vivian wrapped her legs around Max's hips, a tremor shook his body, a reaction she took full advantage of by biting down on his nipple.

"Vivian!" Max roared, pulling her hair to bring her mouth back to his.

He ravished her lips with a new sense of determination. Each plunder of his tongue sent her spiraling back into the unknown. An unfamiliar ache consumed her, begging for relief, yet also yearning for it to never end. Her core stretched below as Max throbbed inside her. She clung to him in anticipation.

Max gritted his teeth. Vivian was determined more than ever to push him past what remained of his sanity. "Dammit, Vivian. Why must you make it difficult for me to redeem myself? You must stop this now."

Vivian's lips lifted into a wicked smile, drawing a groan from Max. "No. I wish for you to ease the ache setting my soul on fire."

Max pulled her hair again and licked across her lips. "You do not hold a clue what you are asking for?"

"Then why don't you show me, Lord Courtland?" Vivian smirked.

Since she arrived back in his life, she had pushed back whenever he declared the boundaries she must abide by. Even now, she forced her need to defy him. And with her wrapped so tightly around him, he was powerless to deny her. If she desired to play with fire, who was he to hold her back from the flames?

Max kissed her with fierce determination. "Consider yourself warned. For I plan to break you into a million pieces you shall never recover from."

Vivian didn't need the warning. She was already aware of how this would compound the heartache she already felt toward Maximilian. Her only response was to kiss him softly on the lips, accepting what fate held in store for her.

Her soft kiss should've gentled his treatment of her. However, it only fed his already out-of-control passion. He pulled out slowly, her wetness guiding him. Then he slammed back into her and pressed in as deeply as he could. Each thrust built into a rhythm that Vivian kept up with by moving in sync. She clung to him, whispering his name over and over as he claimed her soul.

He made good on his promise by sending her over the edge, catching her, and sending her over again. Each time he sent her flying, he captured a part of her soul and stole it into his. She was finally his.

Max increased his pace, chasing his own release to fly with her. Vivian tightened around him and soaked him with her juices, sending him over the edge to sweet oblivion. The vast loneliness he had suffered from after breaking off their betrothal disappeared and filled him with a sense of contentment he had never felt with Vivian before.

Max rolled over and brought Vivian to lie across his chest. His fingers tangled in her hair as he caught his breath. Her husky sigh echoed around him. There was so much he wanted to say but didn't have a clue how to begin. Words of apology rested on the tip of his tongue, but they sounded empty to his own ears. Vivian didn't deserve false sentiments. She needed sincerity—sincerity he didn't deserve to give her.

So he stayed silent, waiting for Vivian to order him out of her bed and demand that he release her from her position. A demand he couldn't by all rights fulfill.

His heart refused to allow it.

Chapter Fifteen

False Rumors

S TARING INTO THE MIRROR, Vivian pinched her cheeks. She had avoided Max throughout the day, but now she must dine with him. He had fulfilled his part of the agreement by spending time with the children. Now she must fulfill her end.

She had watched from the window at his attempt to play with Bennett and Leah in the garden. She thought it would end in a disaster. However, his laughter had mingled with the children's giggles. The sound held a bittersweet emotion for Vivian because she wished it was Max playing with their own children.

When she awakened this morning, she kept envisioning a happily-ever-after with Maximilian. The thoughts only grew her heartache into a flood so substantial it would leave her drowning. Max had made no promises after their lovemaking, an experience that had left her shaken. She had fallen asleep, waiting for him to whisper words of assurance, but his silence held the impact of his warning. He'd left her shattered in a million pieces just as he threatened.

Vivian had hoped he would renege on the agreement. However, when Max returned the children to her care after their tea, Bowers handed her a letter. She sent the children off with a maid to wash while she read the note.

Vivian,

I expect you to fulfill your end of our bargain this evening. Dinner is at seven o'clock.

Max

To anyone who might read the letter, they would read it as a simple request. However, Vivian read the full meaning of his words. Their scandalous interlude from the night before didn't excuse her from fulfilling her obligations.

As the afternoon dragged on, Vivian grew nervous at how Max would treat her since his words held no warmth. Would he mention how he had warmed her bed? Or would he pretend it never happened?

More importantly, how did she want him to react?

The clock struck seven times, and Vivian didn't budge from staring at herself in the mirror. Max was a stickler for arriving at the prompt hour, and Vivian had always been punctual when Max courted her. As she recalled the past, she realized how falsely she had presented herself to him. She had painted a picture of her as a demure debutante who followed every rule of their strict society.

She had never shown him her faults. Like her tendency to never arrive at the correct hour. She only did so with Max because he grew impatient when someone didn't abide by the designated time. She had never wanted to disappoint him. However, now she couldn't care less. Nor did she have to. He obviously held a low opinion of her if his shock at her virginity was anything to go by.

After one last glance in the mirror, Vivian set out for the dining room. When she reached the doorway, Bowers offered her a smile of encouragement. She nodded for him to present her.

Bowers cleared his throat. "Lord Courtland, Lady Vivian has arrived for dinner."

Max watched Vivian sweep into the room as her title demanded. Even though she was now a governess, she still carried herself as a lady. Every servant in the household treated her as such, and he would no longer deny it.

He stood up, paying her the respect she deserved. He thought she presented herself with confidence, but when he stood, her steps faltered at his show of etiquette. When the footman stepped forward to assist her into the chair, Max signaled him away.

Max slid Vivian's chair forward. "Thank you for joining me this evening. It has brought me immense pleasure," Max whispered near Vivian's ear.

Before she left her bedchamber, Vivian swore she wouldn't allow Max to rattle her. However, what one swore and what one was capable of were two entirely different matters. The husky tone of his whisper left Vivian incapable of delivering a snippy response.

Max returned to his seat and waited for the footmen to finish placing the dishes on the table. "That will be all."

Max had made the request earlier with Bowers for the servants to make themselves scarce after they delivered dinner. He didn't need an audience while he dined with Vivian. While Bowers argued over Vivian's reputation, Max promised he would take his advice to heart and behave like a gentleman. Bowers had muttered under his breath about how slim the likelihood would be but followed his orders.

"If you wouldn't mind serving us." Max nodded toward the dishes.

"As you wish, Lord Courtland," Vivian bit out.

If Max intended to remind Vivian how he still considered her a servant, then he made his point clear. While his request wasn't unheard of among his class when a husband required privacy with his wife or mistress, Vivian took his message at face value. He wished to declare their interlude a mistake and one they wouldn't indulge in again. She should feel gratitude for offering them privacy to discuss the delicate subject. Instead, it stung her pride.

Max waited with patience as Vivian filled their plates. He wanted to declare how mistaken she was about his opinion of her. However, Bowers hovered outside the door, ready to protect Vivian if she required his assistance. Her pinched lips and flushed cheeks showed her displeasure with him. And he didn't hold a clue as to why. She couldn't blame him for not talking with her today when she had chosen to avoid him. She had even stayed away when he entertained the children. He had hoped she would join them to help ease the discomfort of the situation. Luckily for him, the children were forgiving in nature and accepted him without hesitation after he played with them.

He saw for himself how Vivian offered valid advice. The children needed reassurance in their time of need. Reassurance he'd been neglectful of because of his own sorrow and the pressure to make the decisions their parents would've wanted. Now, he needed to reassure Vivian of her place in his life.

When she was late to arrive at dinner, Max had worried he'd frightened Vivian away with his advances. He should've awakened her before he slipped from her bed. Instead, he had fled like a coward, ashamed of himself for not believing in her love. He had allowed a close friend to slander Vivian's name and virtue because he had wanted an excuse to break their union. Even when she pleaded her innocence, he had taken the word of a scoundrel instead of the woman he professed to love.

Because of his callous disregard, he'd treated Vivian like a skilled courtesan instead of the innocent lady she was. He should've romanced her the first time with candles and flowers, not claim her roughly. However, it was impossible to recreate the experience for her. For now, his actions moving forward must show Vivian that he loved her.

Max took a sip of wine. "I had a pleasurable afternoon with the children."

Vivian spread the napkin across her lap. "They enjoyed their time with you, too."

"I hoped you would join us."

Vivian played with a spoon, waiting for Max to eat. "You did not make it a requirement in our bargain. So, I assumed you wished only to engage with the children."

Max took a bite instead of replying. While her tone held a snideness, he also heard a hint of sadness. How was he to convince Vivian to lower her guard? Especially when he had mangled her character with his distrust, then with his abrasive behavior at every opportunity when she'd attempted to prove her worthiness as a governess, a position she should've never held if he'd followed through on his commitment to her. But he'd been a fool and showed her he deemed her unworthy.

"Perhaps tomorrow you can join us. They wish to play a game I am unfamiliar with. Pirates and princesses? And something about a treasure map?"

Vivian attempted to hold back a smile but failed at Max's confusion. "You never heard the legend about a band of pirates and princesses hiding a treasure in the hills behind the manor?"

Vivian's grin lit the room, not to mention his heart. Her eyes blazed with animated mischief and, if he wasn't mistaken, a secret.

Max twisted his lips. "My cousin never made mention of this tale."

"Never?" Vivian's lips twisted as she held back her amusement.

"Never."

Vivian shrugged. She didn't elaborate, wanting to keep the air of mystery surrounding the children's game. If Max wished to bond with Bennett and Leah, then she must keep with the suspense. They stayed silent while they ate.

While her brothers and other young gentleman indulged in frivolous activities, Max never did. He always held true to his dignified behavior, never stepping out of line. Why? Especially when Joy behaved as the complete opposite. Even their parents lived life with joyful exuberance. Did he carry a serious demeanor to offset the behavior of his family?

Vivian dabbed her mouth with the napkin. "Then I guess you will learn tomorrow."

Max slid his hand to touch her fingertips. "Does that mean you will join us tomorrow?"

Vivian pulled her hand away before Max realized how her fingers trembled at his slight touch. "If you insist."

Max sighed. "No. I do not insist. I am asking."

Vivian turned her head at Max's soft request. She couldn't decipher the look in his eyes. The smile he sent her way didn't quite match the uncertainty in his gaze. His behavior this evening left her more confused than ever. It was best if she retired for the evening. Perhaps then she could gather her thoughts in order.

Vivian nodded. "Then yes, I will join you and the children tomorrow."

Max's smile widened. "Excellent. Then shall we enjoy dessert in the library?"

"If you do not mind, I am a bit overtired and would like to retire for the evening."

Max could either act the brute and push the demand or he could behave like a gentleman and ease her discomfort. Neither option sounded viable when he would much rather draw her into his arms and plead her forgiveness. However, he wasn't a fool to see she wouldn't welcome any affection from him. He'd noticed her hesitation when she addressed him this evening. Unsure of what he would say, let alone demand. Nor did he want to feud with her. Since her arrival, their behavior had been fraught with tension. So many unspoken words stood between them.

Max rose and offered his hand to help Vivian rise. "Of course. Thank you for your company. I enjoyed dining with someone other than myself." He squeezed her hand and winked at her. "I must admit, I am much of a bore."

Vivian's eyes widened at how Max made a jest about himself. For one who took himself seriously, he'd never shown her this side. She didn't understand what came over her, but she couldn't help herself.

"Yes. You can be at times," Vivian teased.

Max threw his head back and laughed, shocking Vivian even more. She expected a comment bitten back in retaliation. Instead, he only showed his amusement. Who was this gentleman? She quite liked him.

Instead of replying to Vivian's comment, he lifted her hand to his lips and brushed a kiss across her knuckles. Her soft sigh soothed his doubts about how he had overstepped his bounds last night and encouraged him that he might still hold a chance at winning her affection. If he wanted her to love him, then he must stop being the insensitive clod he'd been since he broke their engagement.

He dropped her hand and stepped away from her before he did anything foolish. Like embrace her and ravish her lips. However, there was enough speculation among the servants about his relationship with Vivian. He didn't need to add any more unwanted gossip. He would bide his time when there wasn't a butler standing in the hallway, waiting to interrupt them.

"Pleasant dreams, sweet Vivian."

Max's husky parting words lured Vivian to take a step toward him. The intimacy surrounding them overtook her senses. It didn't help how his brief kiss on her fingers had sent a tingling sensation to her core. Just his touch alone set her soul aflame. His change of character this evening contradicted her musings when she had hesitated to join him for dinner. He had acted the respectful gentleman from when he courted her. Except for when he opened himself to her by showing her glimpses of a character much deeper than she'd known.

Their gazes connected, and Vivian thought she saw hope reflected in his gaze. But it swiftly changed when a throat cleared from behind them.

"Would you like dessert served now, Lord Courtland?" Bowers asked.

Max kept his gaze locked on Vivian. "No. Vivian is retiring for the evening. Please pass on our regrets to the cook. Dinner was scrumptious, and our appetites are full. Tell her we shall eat the dessert tomorrow with the children during afternoon tea."

Bowers nodded. "Very well, my lord." He turned to Vivian and held out some letters. "Please forgive me, my lady. I never delivered these to you today."

Vivian took the letters from Bowers, noticing a letter from her sister. She didn't recognize the handwriting on the other letter. She would learn once she retired to her bedchamber. Vivian smiled in anticipation of reading Chloe's letter.

"Thank you, Bowers." She turned to Max and dropped into a curtsey. "Pleasant evening, my lord."

Max waited until Vivian's footsteps faded along the hallway before addressing Bowers. The butler had his irritating eyebrow quirked at him. Why he felt the need to explain himself to Bowers was beyond him. Yet he attempted to anyway.

"It is her name."

"Mmm," was Bowers only reply.

Max threw his hands into the air. "I suppose I am in the wrong again."

"Only if you do not care how the servants will perceive you speaking only her Christian name," Bowers drawled.

Max wiped his hand across his face in exasperation. He understood the hidden meaning behind the butler's comment. By not placing a "lady" in front of Vivian's name, he might as well have addressed her as Miss Wescott. He could deny the accusation, but it gave him pause to consider if his intentions, by speaking her name, only appeased his confusion about how he viewed her position in his life. Did he still consider her a servant on some level? Or had he fallen into old habits from when he courted her and they spoke each other's name on an intimate level whenever they were alone?

He refused to fall into introspection while in the company of a servant. "Who were the letters from?"

Bowers peered at him with speculation before answering. "One of them was from her sister. The other carried no significant clue of who wrote the letter. I can only tell you it came from London."

Max nodded. Her mother or an acquaintance must have sent her news of London. "That will be all for the evening."

Bowers didn't reply but left Max standing alone in the dining room, wishing he wasn't alone again. While Vivian was so close, she remained out of his reach.

Only for now, though.

Chapter Sixteen

V IVIAN TORE OPEN THE letter and smiled at her sister's handwriting. She missed Chloe and wished she could've brought her along to Scotland. Most people would describe her family's behavior as erratic. Her brothers were foolish scoundrels who spent their lives in one mischievous act after another. And her mother flittered around, ignoring the issues their family faced, while her father lived in denial.

My dearest Vivian,

I received your letter, and I find comfort that you arrived in Scotland safely. I had worried about your journey and your new home. It warms my heart to hear how Lord Courtland is your employer. It is a terrible tragedy, though, of his cousin's death. Those poor children must be heartbroken. At least they have you to help them with their heartache.

In your next letter, please tell me more about the children. Are they delightful to spend time with? Will they journey with Lord Courtland back to London? Will you also attend his sister's wedding? Mother and I saw her at the modiste, and Joy mentioned she invited you to her wedding.

Speaking of Mother, she has not given up on trying to secure tickets to Almack's. Each attempt she makes only causes our family more embarrassment. I wish you were here to dissuade her. She always listens to your calm reason.

Our brothers' behavior has not changed in the slightest. They still carouse the taverns and gaming hells until the early hours of the morning. Then sleep their days away, only to rise and start all over again. Godfrey won a tidy sum to keep them afloat with their nefarious habits.

Father drinks his sorrows away at the club. He stays away all day to avoid Mother's antics on trying to regain their status.

As for myself, I am trying to remain optimistic. At every attempt, I avoid our family and hide away in the library. You know I hide there because of my love of reading, but also because no one else would step foot in there. Which makes it the perfect hiding space. My friends visit me on occasion to fill me in on the whisperings of the ton. While our family's demise remains on their tongues, there are other scandals stealing their attention away. Hopefully, by your return to London, our troubles will be but a distant memory.

I am sorry for writing to you about such sorrowful news. Especially because of the sacrifices you have made for our family. I admire you, dear sister, and I hope to achieve an ounce of your bravery.

I miss you.

Your devoted sister,

Chloe

Vivian sighed, folding the letter. She wished she held an optimistic outlook like her sister, but she understood the dynamics of the ton better than Chloe. She hoped her sister remained naive and never had to endure the harsh realities of their standing in society. However, Chloe's letter showed signs of how her innocence slipped away, something Vivian had hoped to protect. But saving her sister wasn't an option when she struggled to survive. She only prayed in time she could. She didn't know how, but it wouldn't stop her from trying.

An act she'd spent a lifetime attempting but always failing at. With her family's downfall, it had become an impossible feat. One act had caused several more to follow, knocking Vivian back with each failed attempt. With her mother's penchant for shopping and her three brothers' proclivities for gambling, it had led their father to make investments with unscrupulous gentlemen.

The gentlemen gave her father money to invest, and in return, they offered him a sizable profit. However, her father thought to swindle the gentlemen, not realizing the connections these men held. Once the gentlemen discovered her father's betrayal, they sought their retribution.

They spread a tale amongst the ton of his activities. Then they proceeded with their threats by forcing her father to pay them back every coin he stole. Her father had to sell every property that wasn't entailed and wiped away their fortune overnight, which had left her family in shame and dissolute.

Vivian had floated through her courtship with Max, oblivious to her father's activities, imagining she led a pampered, secured life. When in fact, her security was based on greed and false prestige. However, it had also shown her the genuine characteristics of those she loved.

She slid her sister's letter into the drawer of the nightstand and picked up the other letter. Vivian didn't recognize the handwriting, and the seal was plain, with no crest to identify the sender. She peeled it open and read the mysterious letter.

Miss Wescott,

You think you are quite clever by finding positions for your friends and yourself in Scotland. However, do not think for one second the scandal of your actions will not reach the employers you secured. Not only will they learn of your actions, but so will every peer in Scotland who seeks a servant with your qualifications.

You hold the opinion you are untouchable because of the status you once held in society. However, you could not be more mistaken. It is a shame how your friends must suffer because of your superiority. But then your fall from grace has held a dramatic impact these past few months.

I would be lying if I deny how much pleasure that has brought me. I barely contained my laughter when I learned you had taken a position with your former fiancé. A most befitting position you have found yourself in. I cannot imagine Lord Courtland has knowledge of your latest scandal. The poor bloke is probably still reeling from your betrayal.

I send this letter as a warning. When you and your friends least expect it, you will find yourselves ruined to where the only position you will ever find yourselves is on your backs with your legs spread wide open to earn a coin. Perhaps this is how you earn your coins now to save your reputation. It would not surprise me in the slightest.

When you least expect it …

Vivian flipped the page over but found no signature showing who had written the threatening letter. While the letter held more of an opinion on her character and knowledge of her whereabouts, Vivian saw it for the threat it was. She only questioned when it would happen. While the person never signed the letter, it must be Lord Baldridge who threatened Vivian and her friends. He wanted to retaliate against them for the embarrassment they had caused him.

Vivian folded the letter and placed it with her sister's. She rose and paced across the rug, biting her bottom lip. Her employment was contingent until Max found somebody more suitable. Also, her friends' positions were secure. That was, unless the rumor spread to Edinburgh, which the letter stated would be inevitable. Perhaps if she told Max the truth about how she had lost her last position, he might find the compassion to speak with the other families and secure her friends' positions.

However, before she spoke to Max, she needed to speak with her friends first. Tomorrow wasn't an option since she had promised to join Max and the children for tea and treasure hunting in the afternoon. But the day after, she would arrange another outing for the children to play while she discussed the contents of her letter with her friends.

With newfound determination, she went to the desk and wrote out messages to her friends to meet. Once she finished, she set them to the side. She would have Bowers arrange delivery in the morning.

Vivian sent up a prayer that nothing happened in the meantime.

Max trudged along the hallway toward his bedchamber. The evening hadn't ended the way he'd planned. However, it hadn't ended miserably either. In fact, Vivian's gaze before Bowers interrupted them gave him hope.

He pushed open the door to his room and stripped off his clothes. Max had given instructions to his valet not to bother him until he requested his assistance. He didn't want the man to interrupt an intimate interlude between Vivian and him. A wishful thought on his part.

After he disrobed to his trousers, he noticed the candlelight shining from underneath the doorway leading to Vivian's room. He pressed his ear against the panel and heard a soft rustling sound and Vivian muttering. He reached for the doorknob but stopped himself before he walked inside and interrupted her privacy.

Max wanted Vivian's trust and to repair their relationship. To achieve that outcome, he couldn't lord his position around. Even if he ached to spend every minute with her. To wrap her in his embrace and place soft kisses on her lips. To hold her next to him while they slipped away into their dreams. No. He must remain behind the door and lie in his bed by himself.

Alone.

Tomorrow he would attempt to prove himself to Vivian and win her affection. He had wronged her, and he needed to prove himself worthy of her love.

He hoped nothing more prevented his pursuit.

Chapter Seventeen

False Rumors

TWO DAYS LATER, VIVIAN hurried across the lush green grass of the park, anxious to reach her friends. She wouldn't have long to spend with them before they returned to their employers.

She arrived late because she had spent the morning reassuring the children they would return in time for their afternoon tea. Bennett and Leah worried they would miss their visit with Max. They had shared an exciting adventure with him yesterday, looking for missing treasure, and they wanted to enjoy more fun with him.

She understood the urgency because she wanted to experience the same. The day before, he had acted like the Max she had fallen in love with. Not the arse who had broken her heart. She didn't even ponder the sudden change in his behavior, only how much her heart opened toward him. However, she did question why he hadn't seduced her after they put the children to bed. Did he regret making love to her?

Vivian shook her thoughts away. Dwelling on Max's regard was an unwanted distraction when she had more pressing matters to attend to.

"Go play with the other children," Vivian urged Bennett and Leah.

She rushed over to her friends after the children ran toward their play-mates. She didn't want to frighten them with the letter she had received, but their expressions of fear matched her own. A letter lay upon each of their laps that appeared identical to hers. She was unsure of their contents but knew they held the same threat.

"You each received a letter of your own?" Vivian asked.

Her friends nodded.

"May I read them?" Vivian held out her hand for the letters.

She read through each letter. The same threat was visible, but each letter held information only the receiver would be privy to. Whoever wrote the letters had intimate knowledge of her friends, which had triggered the fear in their expressions.

"What should we do?" Sara's voice trembled.

"We do nothing. We allowed them to threaten us in England, but we will not allow them to threaten us here in Scotland," Grace answered with confidence.

"You and Sara can speak with confidence because of your standing with your employers. The rest of us do not hold that advantage," Flora ranted. "Vivian's livelihood rests on the whim of a gentleman who threw her over instead of trusting the love they held, which only proves the lord never loved Vivian to begin with. Even now, he fools her into imagining they can share more. And I hover on the brink of losing a position I never truly held. I have no security since my employer has yet to arrive with his children for me to care for. My situation has not improved since I arrived in Edinburgh."

Vivian crinkled her eyebrows. "What do you mean, your employer has never arrived in Scotland?"

"My employer has yet to arrive. I spend my days walking around town with no purpose. Of course, I do not differ from the other servants. We wonder how much longer we will hold our positions before someone dismisses us," Flora explained.

"Why have you not shared this with us earlier?" Vivian asked.

Flora sighed. "At first, it overwhelmed me to return to Scotland. Now I only grow worrisome. Before long, my family will learn of my return to Scotland, and they will force me to wed a groom of their choosing. I hoped the mess from London would have cleared, and we could return. But now with this threat hovering over our heads, I fear my destiny is to wed a Scottish heathen who I hold no affection for."

Vivian winced at Flora's predicament. When she set out on this course, Vivian hadn't predicted this for their outcomes. She had failed her friends yet again. And she didn't hold a clue about how to rectify their situations. She must confide in Maximilian and ask for his help. Surely, after the intimacy they shared, he wouldn't hesitate to help her with the trouble she had landed her and her friends in.

"I am scared," Sara whispered.

Vivian wrapped her arms around her friend. "Give me time to figure out a solution, and I promise to make this right. I hold remorse for the position I have placed us in."

"May I ask how you plan to fix this?" Grace scoffed. "No offense, but you can plead your case to Lord Courtland and seek his forgiveness and find yourself in a position only the rest of us can dream about."

"Grace, do not be so hard on Vivian. She has done nothing but help us." Sara defended Vivian.

"Help us? She is the very reason we are stuck in the middle of godforsaken nowhere. I never wanted to return to Scotland, let alone have to worry when I might lose my position. These threats only guarantee not if but when," Flora declared.

Grace and Flora rose to gather the children before Vivian had a chance to defend herself and ask for their patience. Vivian's heart bled for her friends from the truth of Grace's and Flora's words. Their destinies differed from her own, all because of the position they were born into in the hierarchy of life.

"Do not think too harshly of them. The letters have scared them. They value your friendship and only need reassurance." Sara comforted Vivian from Grace's and Flora's harsh words.

Vivian nodded, attempting to keep her tears at bay. Her life spiraled out of her control, and she had nobody to turn to.

Sara stood and bent over to hug Vivian. "I will wait to hear from you. Note this, we all hold faith in you."

Sara gathered her charge, leaving Vivian to watch Leah and Bennett chasing after each other. The visit with her friends today had ended more dramatically than she had expected. She had hoped to reassure them, and instead, she left feeling defeated.

Grace and Flora weren't at fault for any resentment toward her. Because once again, they faced an unstable future, leaving them in fear of the unknown. While Sara held an optimistic view and had faith in her, her other two friends understood the threat at stake. The outcome awaiting them was the same one before Vivian had found them employment in Scotland.

A future Vivian swore she would protect them from.

Max wandered toward the nursery instead of settling the last of his cousin's affairs. The draw to spend time with Vivian before they returned to London consumed his every thought, especially after their amusing afternoon with the children yesterday. The children had been excited when she provided eye patches for their treasure hunt. When she handed over his, he noted the handiwork of her sewing, which explained the light shining from underneath her door the night before.

Vivian had regaled them with a tale about pirates hiding their treasure and handed them each a map with clues. She'd swept Max along for the thrilling adventure. He admired the effort she had made to make the scene believable. She had even shocked him when the children found a treasure. She had filled a small chest with trinkets only a child would enjoy. The smiles on the children's faces made it all worthwhile. He now understood what Vivian meant about what Bennett and Leah needed more than anything else. A sense of familiarity and compassion. But most of life's adventures.

To continue with their sense of family, the children joined them for dinner. And with this meal, no one spilled any drinks or shed any tears. After Leah fell asleep listening to Vivian read a book and he carried her to bed, Max felt an overwhelming need to kiss Vivian as he watched her tuck the children into bed. However, he refrained with what remained of his self-control. Because he didn't want her to see him as a lustful lord who was unable to keep his hands off the lovely servant.

When he couldn't find Vivian or the children, he retraced his steps downstairs in search of Bowers. He found the butler giving instructions to a footman. He waited for the butler's attention. Max didn't want to give the servants room to gossip about his interest in Vivian.

Bowers cleared his throat. "How may I assist you, Lord Courtland?"

"Where are Miss Wescott and the children? I cannot find them in the house, and Vivian should be teaching them their lessons." His tone came out harsher than he intended.

Bowers arched his brow, assuming the worst of Max's intention to locate Vivian. "Lady Vivian has taken the children into Edinburgh to play at the park."

Max scoffed. "Why did she travel into town for that enjoyment? There is enough land on the estate for the children to run wild."

"Perhaps because she wished for the enjoyable companionship of her friends and it gives the children an opportunity to play with other children their age." Bowers's tone emphasized his need to defend Vivian.

"What friends? She hasn't had any opportunity to make friends."

"I believe they are her friends from London, my lord," Bowers responded.

The butler's answer only confused Max. He knew for a fact that every friend Vivian had had turned their backs on her. Everyone except for his sister, Joy. Who would seek her company in Edinburgh?

"Do you know the ladies' names so I might call upon their fathers?" asked Max.

"They are not members of the peerage. They are ladies who befriended her while she was a governess in England. They, too, have also found governess positions in Edinburgh. She traveled with them from London," Bowers explained.

"Why would her friends follow her to Edinburgh?"

"I cannot rightly say, my lord."

Max quirked an eyebrow. "Cannot or will not?"

Bowers didn't answer Max. "Is there anything else I can help you with, Lord Courtland?"

It would be pointless to interrogate the butler when Bowers had no intention of revealing anything about Vivian. Since the servant disliked how Max treated and addressed her, Bowers would make it difficult for Max to learn anything. His only option was to question the source herself. It irritated him how, after they spent the day together; she felt she could neglect her duties as a governess by not teaching the children their lessons.

Vivian's past traits of being frivolous with her time showed again today. He thought they had moved forward, but after her absence this morning with the children, he realized he had lost his footing and didn't know how to regain himself. If he railed at her when she returned, they would find themselves in the same predicament. Leah would cry and Bennett would want to throw stones at him to defend Vivian's honor. Not to mention how the servants would ignore him.

He needed to find a happy medium with Vivian or else they'd keep twirling in the same circle, around and around, growing dizzy because they couldn't find common ground. Before he confronted Vivian, he must answer the questions plaguing him. Did he want something lasting with Vivian? Or did he entertain the thought of her to ease his loneliness and sorrow?

He trudged back to the study to finish his cousin's paperwork. Max almost had Seamus's affairs in order. They needed to leave for London in a few days to attend his sister's wedding. That was his reason for searching for Vivian, to share the wonderful news with her and surprise her.

Max looked up and noted the time. It had only been half an hour since he left his conversation with Bowers when he heard Bennett and Leah running along the hallway. Vivian had returned in time for the children's afternoon tea. He stood and moved to the front of the desk as he waited for Vivian and the children. The children came running inside the study without Vivian, chattering excitedly about their time at the park.

His irritation pricked at how Vivian didn't accompany the children. Was she under the assumption that if she hid, he would excuse her behavior for the day? While he should be furious about her neglecting the children's lessons, he was more disappointed that she didn't join them. Because he wanted to gaze upon her lovely smile.

Before he could question the children on Vivian's whereabouts, Bowers directed the maid where to set the tray holding their afternoon respite. The maid poured the tea, while the children filled their plates with biscuits. They sat on the settee waiting for his lead before they began eating. He smiled at them and nodded, giving them permission to start.

While he wished to question where Vivian was, it wasn't fair to the children. Vivian's absence spoke volumes. He rubbed at his chest, wishing for the hopelessness to fade away.

A wish he feared would never come true.

Chapter Eighteen

V IVIAN SAT AT THE table, waiting for Max to arrive for dinner. The children had eaten earlier and retired to bed. They had an exhausting day playing at the park and their time spent with Max this afternoon. Leah and Bennett had chattered nonstop throughout their dinner about how Max had taken them riding. A footman had joined their fun, each man holding a child on their horse as they traveled over their land.

It would appear Max had redeemed himself in the children's eyes. Bennett hero-worshipped him, and if Vivian wasn't mistaken, young Leah held a crush on Max, which didn't surprise her in the slightest because Vivian still held her own crush on the lord. Who did she fool? She was hopelessly in love with him. Always had been and always would be. No matter how much he broke her heart.

"I thought I would be dining alone this evening," Max drawled as he strode into the dining room.

Vivian smiled with patience, a trait she would need this evening. While Max was a proud man, he was also a sensitive one, a characteristic she now understood. She had bruised his ego by not joining the children this afternoon. Also, Bowers had warned her of Max's displeasure at taking the children away from their studies again. She would need to smooth over her actions before she begged for his help.

"Since you continue to honor my request, I will continue to honor yours." Vivian folded her hands in her lap.

She wished to smooth away the frown from Max's lips, a right she would've held if he had ever trusted her. And her actions gave him no reason to trust her now. Still, it didn't stop her from yearning for any shared affection. She wanted nothing more than for Max to wrap her in his embrace and soothe her worries away. She held on to foolish wishes.

Max signaled the footman to serve the meal. They ate the first two courses in silence. Vivian kept peeking at Max from under her eyelashes, but he never once glanced her way that she was aware of. It didn't help her nerves any. She had decided this afternoon to discuss her dilemma with Max, but with each minute ticking away in silence, her nerve swiftly vanished away.

Something troubled Vivian, but Max held no clue about the source. Was it the reason for visiting her friends? Also, why hadn't she joined the children this afternoon?

She kept darting glances at him in between bites. While he pretended indifference at her company, he was anything but. He wished they didn't have to suffer through the pretense of proper manners and he could dismiss the servants. But he'd already caused enough room for gossip about Vivian, and he promised himself he wouldn't subject her to anything more. He only had to endure another course and dessert. Then he would plead his excuse for finishing paperwork. Once the servants retired for the evening, he would knock on Vivian's door.

Only to learn what troubled her, nothing more. However, the thought of being alone with her sent his mind racing with scandalous images of Vivian standing before him in her nightgown. He groaned inwardly. He didn't need his desires to flare for Vivian's sake. Did she even realize how tempting she was in her cloak of vulnerability? She kept biting on her bottom lip to stop herself from speaking with him.

While he wondered what she wanted to discuss, he also hoped she stayed silent. If not, then he couldn't resist holding her in his arms while she spilled her troubles. During their horse ride this afternoon, the children had innocently informed Max about how Vivian had fought with her friends and how she had wiped away her tears on the carriage ride back home. This led Max to believe she'd neglected the children's lessons because something troubled Vivian enough to seek her friend's companionship to ease her burdens. But if what the children divulged was true, her friends didn't help solve her problem but added to it instead.

"Lord Courtland," Vivian whispered. When he never responded, Vivian darted a glance at the servants to see if they paid them attention. "Max," she whispered louder.

Max closed his eyes at her whisper. Damn. Now she forced him to acknowledge her. He opened his eyes, his gaze clashing with hers. When he noticed the desperation pouring from her depths, he silently swore his frustration. Damn their predicament. A predicament they were in, because of his foolish reaction months ago. If only he had believed in her, she would be his wife, not a governess he employed who he was forbidden to show affection toward.

He must pull himself together. Max turned in her direction with a smile. "Yes, Miss Wescott?"

"I need to discuss a matter with you," Vivian continued whispering.

Max noticed Vivian kept darting glances toward the servants while she tried to get his attention. Whatever she wanted to discuss must be personal, which meant she didn't wish to discuss his wards but them. A matter he was still conflicted about.

Max jumped in his seat when her fingertips brushed across his hand resting on the table. It shocked him how his body reacted to her mere touch. If he were any wiser, he would've pulled his hand away, instead of capturing her hand in his grasp. To hell with the servants. They weren't even his, and he grew tired of their insolence toward him.

"That will be all, Matthews. Please have Bowers set up the dessert and tea in the library," Max ordered.

Vivian tried to tug her hand out of Max's grasp, but he held firm. He rubbed his thumb back and forth across her knuckles in a slow memorizing motion that hypnotized her and drew her under his spell. As she watched the gentle caress, her body relaxed, and she leaned toward him.

Max smiled to himself, pleased that Vivian wasn't as indifferent to him as she pretended to be. He rose and tugged Vivian to her feet. "Shall we?"

Vivian pierced Max with a puzzled look, unclear what he meant. However, instead of questioning him, she followed him by his side to the library. He led her to the settee before returning to close the door. If she wasn't mistaken, she swore he turned the key in the handle to lock them inside.

Max strode back to her with purpose to his step. His confidence should've been a warning, but Max had caught Vivian under his spell and she admired how his body moved so fluidly with his swagger. Not to mention how his gaze kept her frozen, waiting for him.

He never gave Vivian a chance to question his actions. He swept her into his arms and ravished her mouth with a hunger out of his control. Max craved the sweetness clinging to her succulent lips. His tongue teased them to part to invade her mouth and savor the delectable taste of Vivian. He inhaled each whimper escaping from her throat. They were balms to his soul.

Vivian rewarded his attention by wrapping her arms around his neck and tugging him closer. Her whimpers soon turned into greedy moans that inflamed the passion surrounding them. Max grabbed her hips and pressed his cock against her core. The damn garments separating them urged him to slide the buttons of her dress undone. In his impatience, he ripped the garment, tearing a slit along the seam.

Vivian should've put a halt to Max's seduction when she heard the material of her gown rip apart. It wasn't what she meant when she told him she had something to discuss with him. She wanted to confide in him about her troubles. However, one touch from Max and she was powerless to deny her desire for him. He made her feel safe and secure in his arms.

Vivian lowered her hands and tugged at his cravat until it came undone. Her fingers frantically attempted to undress him. Her body craved the touch of him against hers. She needed his warmth to soothe her troubles away. To have him caress her body to fevered heights and kiss her until she slipped away into the fantasy of them being together as one forever.

Vivian's urgency matched his own. With each piece of discarded clothing, they burned kisses upon each other, fueling his need to claim her again. After he stripped her dress away, he lifted her to straddle him as he sat down. He pulled her hair back and sucked on her neck, inhaling her desire.

"Maximilian." Vivian's husky whisper filled the air.

Max pulled Vivian's hand down to the placket of his trousers. "Undo them."

There was no hesitation in Vivian as she followed his demand.

"Now pull out my cock. It aches for your soft caress," he ordered.

Vivian wrapped her hand around Max's cock, and the power of his desire pulsed a steady beat under her closed fingers.

Max groaned in her ear. "That's it, love, stroke it nice and slow."

Max swore he had died and gone to heaven with each pull of her grip. Her strokes grew bolder each time he groaned his pleasure in her ear. When her thumb brushed his wetness around the tip of his cock, he thought he would explode from the sheer ecstasy of her touch. His hand lowered and slid into her curls, sinking into her wetness.

He stroked her clit, brushing back and forth until it hardened tight with her need. "Ahh, you are such a naughty girl, my sweet Vivian. Stroking my cock makes you wet."

A stirring rippled through Vivian at Max's scandalous words. They spoke so true of how her body responded to please him. She should feel ashamed of her wanton desires, yet Max empowered her as only a goddess could be.

When he slid his fingers inside her, Vivian bit her lip to keep from screaming her pleasure. Her body ached with an uncontrollable passion she needed release from. She shifted her hips in rhythm with his finger, which only intensified the ache. Her grip tightened around him, and she stroked Max faster.

"Yes, sweet Vivian, ride the wave of pleasure. Take what you want and I will fulfill your greatest desires."

Vivian pressed down on Max's hand as she fell apart and splintered into a million pieces. She wanted to cry from the sheer exquisite bliss. However, Max was far from done loving her. Before she drew in a breath, he untangled her hand from around his cock and surged inside her.

As he filled her, Vivian gasped and then soon purred. Max's hands tightened around her waist and guided her on how to move on him. When she stared down at him, his eyelids lowered, and he threw his head back against the cushion as his body thrust up into hers. In this position, he relented the power of their lovemaking to her. While he dominated her senses with the sheer power of his body, he allowed her the power of their dynamics. Hope blossomed in Vivian at his act.

Max opened his eyes and gazed into Vivian's aqua depths, sparkling with an emotion that should scare Max. Instead, it gave him a sense of lightness in his soul he hadn't felt in forever. He drew her hips still and watched her eyes darken with a need so profound it shook him. Yet it didn't scare him one bit.

He lifted his hands and speared them into her hair, dragging her lips to his. With one swipe of his mouth against hers, she pulled him under the waves with her. He drowned in her kisses, never once wanting to breathe anything but her. As much as he desired to ravage her body, he wanted to show Vivian she held the power to destroy him just as much as he did her.

His lips trailed a path of fire along her neck to her breasts. Vivian bit her bottom lip as she watched his tongue circle her nipple before drawing it between his lips. His teeth scraped across the sensitive bud, easing the ache with gentle licks before he sucked down hard. Vivian writhed on Max's cock, causing another sensation of pleasure to ripple through her. Max chuckled at how her body reacted.

He peeked up at her as he suckled on her nipples, watching her eyes grow heavy with desire. Her tongue slid out and licked across her bottom lip, causing Max's cock to harden with an ache demanding release. Her wetness dripped from her pussy, coating his cock with her own demand.

His kisses trailed back to her lips, where he teased his tongue along her bottom lip to soothe the damage she had inflicted with her need. At her soft moan, he kissed across her cheek to her ear and dragged her earlobe through his teeth, biting it gently.

"Please ride me, love," his tantalizing whisper begged. "Fast and hard."

Vivian tightened her fingers around his shoulders, holding on to Max as his body urged hers to lose control. All it took was one press of his cock inside her for her to lose what sanity remained between them. Her fingernails dug into his rigid muscles as she rose and sank down, grinding her pussy against him. His groans and muttered expletives encouraged Vivian along. With each rise, her nipples scraped against his chest, heightening Vivian's senses.

The ache inside Vivian spiraled around and around, spinning faster as she came undone. Max captured her scream in a kiss that left her as shaken as the joining of their two bodies as one. His body shuddered against her as they collapsed against the cushion from the dizzying effect of their lovemaking. She rested her head on his shoulder, drawing in one deep breath after another.

Max wrapped his arms around Vivian, holding her close to his heart before she came to her senses and separated from him. Their lovemaking had left a profound effect on him. He didn't know if he would ever recover if Vivian never opened her heart to him. The emotions demanding attention proved what a fool he'd been for his treatment of her. Would he ever feel worthwhile with Vivian again? Or would his past behavior always be a factor between them?

Vivian pulled away with a blush spreading across her body. She pushed at his chest for him to release her, but it only made Max pull her against him tighter.

"Don't." Max heard the desperation in his voice as he begged her not to move.

She might've settled against him, but she stayed tense. He caressed her body with a soft touch, whispering across her skin until she relaxed. However, the sigh she released let him know she wanted to put distance between them. To keep his conscience aware of her feelings, he placed a kiss against her temple and dropped his arms.

Max's reluctance to release her struck a punch to her soul. However, to protect her heart, she needed to separate herself from him. To stay wrapped in his arms gave Vivian a false sense of happiness she couldn't allow. While she hoped for a happily-ever-after with Maximilian Courtland, the reality of her position as a servant rang clear.

She could be nothing more.

Chapter Nineteen

VIVIAN ROSE OFF MAX, pulling the straps of her chemise up and over her shoulder. Another blush spread across Vivian once she realized they still wore half their clothing. She stepped back, looking for her dress. She pulled it on, but the torn garment prevented her from covering her chest. Max had ripped more than the material. Her buttons were missing, too.

Max winced at Vivian's dilemma. With his lust guiding his actions, he had ruined her dress. He quickly put himself to rights, buttoning his trousers and pulling his shirt over his head. He snagged his suit coat off the floor and draped it over Vivian's shoulders.

Vivian slid her arms through the sleeves. "Thank you," she whispered.

Max stepped back from her, fighting the need to draw her back into his arms. "I apologize. Please allow me to purchase you a new dress when we return to London."

Vivian shook her head. "No. I should be able to repair it."

Max wanted to persuade her to accept his offer but understood pride stood in their way. With the tilt of her chin and her firm answer, she displayed how she viewed them. It didn't matter how they had torn each other's clothes off and fulfilled their deepest desires half an hour ago.

She didn't trust him.

Vivian gathered Max's coat closer around her as she moved to stare out the window. She needed to put some distance between them because he still held the ability to rattle her senses. She longed to unburden herself in his arms. However, she saw this evening for what it was. No matter how he touched or kissed her, it didn't change the circumstances of her situation.

Max stared down at the top of his Hessians, trying to deal with the predicament he found himself in. He wanted to offer for Vivian's hand in marriage, but she would misconstrue his intentions. His desire to marry her was because he loved her and wished never to live another day without her. But she would assume he made his offer because he had ruined her. From this day forth, until he could convince her otherwise, he must keep his hands to himself. No matter how tempting he found her.

A piece of paper on the floor caught his attention. When he picked it up, he noticed it was a letter addressed to Vivian, but with no returning signature. He should respect her privacy, but some alarming words caught his eye. Before he could finish reading the letter, Vivian snatched it out of his hand.

"How dare you!"

"What is the letter about?"

They spoke at the same time. Vivian crumpled the letter in her hand and shoved it into the pocket of her dress. Now, when faced with being able to confide in Max, she changed her mind. He already held a low opinion of her, and after bedding him twice, she showed him no reason to help her. He would probably dismiss her on the spot. Then she couldn't help her friends.

"'Tis nothing. I bid you good evening, Lord Courtland." Vivian tried to step around him.

However, Max refused to let her out of his sight until she explained the contents of the threatening letter. He grabbed her arm and guided her to a chair near the window. He pulled a chair up next to her, blocking any path of an escape. Vivian crossed her arms and looked everywhere but at him.

Max sighed. "I am not your enemy, Vivian. I only want to help. Trust me."

Vivian glared at him. "Trust you. I will trust you the same way you trusted me."

Max leaned back in the chair. "Do you wish to discuss that particular subject now? Because we can. I am more than ready. Are you?"

Vivian bit her tongue, fighting back the urge to unleash her heartache at his feet. But she refused to give him the advantage. In all honesty, she feared the outcome because he still believed the lies.

Max watched the indecision cross over her features. He saw the doubt reflected in her gaze. Doubts he wanted to reassure her no longer mattered, but even he understood it was an inappropriate time. Vivian had another urgent matter that needed his attention and, if he wasn't mistaken, his help.

Max swiped his hand down his face. "Explain the letter."

Vivian didn't understand her reasons for confiding in him. If it was from her friends' distress or the love she held for Max. Or if it was from the loneliness of her isolation from everyone she loved. Or a mixture of them all.

"As you are aware, I gained employment as a governess in London. While working for a family, I made friends with three girls while our charges played in the park. During this time, they welcomed me into their bond of friendship," Vivian began. "My friend Sara came alone to the park one day in tears. Her employer had attempted to accost her, and she ran from him. She was afraid to return to the lord's home."

"My God," Max muttered. Vivian didn't need to fill in the details of the girl's assault for Max to understand the girl's fear. It would be the gentleman's word over hers.

"Thankfully, Sara avoided his clutches but not before his wife came upon them and threw accusations at her. Calling her a strumpet and an unfit employee. Their treatment shocked Sara. You must understand that she is an innocent and, unfortunately, very naive. She is one of those kind souls who believe there is only goodness in everyone," Vivian explained.

"Then why the threatening letter?" Max asked.

Vivian lowered her eyes and played with the button on his coat. The next part she found difficult to share. It was because of her grand scheme to seek revenge that she'd hurt her friends. She realized now it wasn't only Lord Baldridge's actions that had caused her to act out. But how she felt toward the society that'd once welcomed her but now snubbed her in shame. Her selfishness had landed her in this predicament. However, she would sacrifice herself for her friends' secure futures.

"Because I convinced my friends to seek revenge on the lord in question."

Max narrowed his gaze. "How so?"

Vivian raised her chin. "We snuck into a ball, and I ripped off his hairpiece in front of his peers and embarrassed him by slaying his character. I told everyone present how he accosted a governess in his household. One he had offered protection to, by everyone except himself. Then I punched him below the stomach before I walked away."

"Which left him the laughingstock in society. You not only shamed him but his entire family."

Vivian twisted a button off the coat. "Which, in return, left us without positions and unable to find employment. Not even any shopkeepers would hire us."

Max folded his hands together across his stomach. "Which explains your arrival in Scotland. Far enough away from where any rumors would have spread. Bowers mentioned you meeting your friends in the park. I assume these are the same friends and they also sought positions in Scotland. Am I correct?"

Vivian nodded. "At my guidance, I convinced them to. After failure upon failure to secure any positions, my friends grew despaired. I found them positions in Edinburgh after finding mine. They all agreed to make the journey or else fall victim to using their bodies to make money."

"Which member of the peerage did you slander?"

Vivian winced. "Lord Baldridge."

Max hid his disgust at what awaited the ladies if their present employers learned of their deception. There were no options for a woman without a protector. It angered him how Vivian's father and brothers didn't provide her with the security she needed. Instead, she sacrificed herself for them. They did not differ from the reprobates of Lord Baldridge's character, each of them satisfying their vices at the expense of innocents.

"Lord Baldridge does not strike me as a fellow to threaten you and your friends. However, he has his pride. But I do not believe he holds the capability of such an elaborate threat. Especially since he knows how you might respond to him if given a chance. Also, his wife seems too insipid of a lady to write to you. You must have angered someone who holds a personal connection to Lord and Lady Baldridge," Max mused.

"Who, though? The person also sent letters to my friends. Their fear lies at my feet. I have the means to recover, but they are alone and I have failed them by bringing them to Scotland."

Max leaned over and unclenched Vivian's hand. He slid the button out of her grip and traced his finger over the indentation of the holes on her palm. "Give me their names and the names of their employers and I will secure their positions."

Vivian's heart clenched at his gentle caress and the promise he made to protect her friends. It was bittersweet how he responded as a husband to her worries, when he was only a lover who wanted to act the hero. However, she had no other option but to allow him to help her friends.

"Do you believe you can help? Or once the other families learn the truth, they will shun them, too? If so, how will my friends survive?"

Max lifted her palm and placed a kiss in the center. Then he laid her hand back in her lap and sat back. "Then I shall help them find positions either in my household or with another family who would hold sympathy for their situations."

"Why?"

That one word held more questions than he was prepared to answer. So he answered the only one to pacify her for the moment. To answer the full depth of why, he needed to take care of a few matters before he apologized for his behavior over the past year.

Max smirked. "Perhaps because I wish to earn your favor."

Vivian narrowed her gaze. "For what purpose?"

Max's smirk turned to a wicked smile. "My pleasure. Why else?"

Max meant to distract Vivian with his wicked smile and scandalous suggestion, but he didn't fool her for a second. She would let him avoid her question for now, but as soon as her friends' safety was secure from any threats, then she must demand an explanation. Because no matter how much her heart enjoyed his attention, it also yearned for the impossible. And for her to keep her sanity and what pride she had remaining, she must put a stop to whatever this was between them.

"Why else, indeed?" Vivian rose from the chair, slipping the button into the pocket of the suit coat. She would repair his coat along with her dress once she retired to her bedchamber.

Max rose. "May I keep the letter? I would like to show proof when I discuss the situation with the other families who your friends hold positions with."

Vivian withdrew the letter from her pocket and handed it over to Max. "Thank you."

Max waited until Vivian reached the door before he delivered his news. "I will settle this matter tomorrow. We shall return to London at the end of the week. Please prepare the children for the journey."

Vivian paused. What did this mean for her? "I will help the maid pack for the children."

"You are making the return, too," Max declared but withheld the true reason.

Vivian wanted to turn around and pelt Max with questions about her future, but she feared what he might say. She would wait until their return to London to find out what he required of her. She couldn't abandon the children until Max reassured her of their care. However, once Max found her replacement, Vivian feared she would never recover from her heartache this time around.

Vivian never responded to his declaration, only swept out of the library with as much dignity as one could with a dress destroyed and wearing his suit coat. Max ran his hand through his hair and paced back and forth. He'd made a fine mess of Vivian's return to his life. An even bigger one than when he'd dismissed her earlier in the year. She found herself threatened with a predicament she should've never been party to if he had married her like he had promised to.

Tomorrow he would seek the families who employed her friends and secure promises for them. Then he would insist on Vivian meeting her friends to tell them of the promises and to contact him if the families didn't hold true. He wanted them to understand he would help protect them from the evils of society. It wasn't his intent to make himself a knight in shining armor to win Vivian's love. He only wanted to offer them peace of mind. However, if it played to his advantage, he wouldn't find fault with it.

He needed all the help he could get.

Chapter Twenty

V IVIAN SMILED AS THE children played a game of checkers.

Max had yet to return from town. She waited to hear how his discussions went with her friends' employers. A severe rainstorm had swept in after luncheon and continued with its destructive high winds. Max must've stayed at his cousin's club until it was dry. He wouldn't risk riding through the storm because of how his cousin and his wife lost their lives. Max would take precautions to keep Bennett and Leah from suffering any more loss.

Soon, afternoon tea turned into dinnertime. And before long, she had the children nestled in bed. Still, the rain continued to fall, and Max hadn't returned. Vivian decided to wait for Max in the library. She found a book to read and settled on the settee. Instead of her reading, her thoughts filled with images of them loving each other the night before. Her fingers stroked the cushions, searching for what remained of Max's warmth. A silly notion, but at this point, Vivian was desperate to form any connection with Max.

Vivian grew tired while she waited. The book held no interest for her. She stretched out and cushioned her head with a decorative pillow. The flames flickering in the fireplace lured her eyes to close. She promised herself she would only rest for a few minutes, and if Max didn't return soon, she would go to bed.

However, Vivian fell into a deep sleep.

Max covered Vivian with a blanket before settling in a chair opposite her. A quick trip into town had ended with him spending the day at his cousin's club because of the rain pelting the countryside. He would've risked riding through the rain if his cousin hadn't only just perished in the same manner because of their urgency to return home to their children. If he was capable, he would prevent Bennett and Leah from suffering any more heartache. Once the rain turned to a slight drizzle, he had returned to his cousin's home.

He wanted to wake Vivian and share his news with her. He assumed she waited in the library to discuss his visit to town. However, he didn't have the heart to wake her. She had stayed awake late the night before sewing again. When he returned to his bedchamber after eating breakfast, his suit coat had lain on his bed with the button sewn back on.

Lying on top of the coat was a note with her friends' names and the families they'd taken positions with. Max was familiar with two families. He had talked with Lord Lockhart and Lord Somerville recently at the club. The third family he was unfamiliar with. After a few inquiries, he'd learned the household waited for the heir to arrive. He'd arranged for the other gentlemen to look after Miss Grant if her position proved a failure.

Now, he needed to correct his mistakes with the lady who lay sleeping peacefully before him. He'd prepared letters to help her family reposition themselves in society. He even considered paying her father's debt. Her father's deceit over their financial situation had caused her family's fall from grace. Lord Wescott spent his days drinking at his club, instead of regaining financial stability for his family. Vivian's father was under the assumption that if he ignored their troubles, they would fix themselves on their own. Which explained why Vivian had sought employment.

He understood her reasoning. Her seeking employment was her family's only salvation, and she did so for one reason only. So her sister didn't have to suffer. It disgusted him how her brothers didn't take responsibility to support their family. However, they differed no more than their father and continued with their hedonistic lifestyles. Their mother wasn't innocent either. She spent money as if she were the queen herself. How Vivian and her sister came from the same family astounded him.

Max remembered the first time he saw Vivian after she entered society. She had left him a speechless fool with her dazzling smile and her sparkle-filled eyes. She differed so much from the other debutantes, which was probably the reason he'd grown so smitten with her. Vivian never hesitated to voice her opinion of the less fortunate and befriended every wallflower. She never flaunted how every gentleman wanted to dance with her. No. She made excuses and convinced the gentleman to dance with one of her friends instead.

So it hadn't surprised him when she confessed to him about defending her friend from Lord Baldridge. In her naivety, she had failed to understand how society would seek revenge and leave Vivian and her friends destitute just because they held the power. While she acted out of the goodness of her heart, it had placed her in a vulnerable position she might never recover from.

When Vivian arrived, he'd been furious at Joy's interference. But now, he held gratitude for his sister for bringing Vivian back into his life. He wanted the girl he fell in love with, but he feared he had destroyed her. When Joy married Bradley, he hoped he would rejoice with his own happiness. Max longed to bring back Vivian's dazzling smile and sparkling eyes.

Only time would tell if he succeeded.

Vivian stretched, her muscles stiff. She sat up quickly, realizing where she'd slept throughout the night. The sun peered through the window, and the rays dried the wet landscape. She looked down to see a blanket tangled around her limbs. Had Max returned and covered her? If so, why hadn't he woken her?

"Max?"

"Over here."

Vivian's gaze traveled across the library, searching for him. She found him squatted near the corner shelves, sliding a book back onto the shelf. She gulped at how his trousers molded over his powerful thighs. When he rose and pulled down his vest, she couldn't avert her eyes even if she wanted to. He was a splendid specimen that made her mouth water.

Vivian cleared her throat. "When did you make it back?"

Max leaned his arm on a shelf. "A few hours ago."

"Why did you let me continue to sleep?"

Max shrugged. "I enjoyed watching you rest."

"Maximilian." Vivian blushed, saying his name as a reprimand.

Max smiled at her discomfort. "You are a lovely sight to gaze upon in the morning."

Vivian was powerless to resist Max when he attempted to charm her. There were many facets to Max's character, and his charming nature undid her every time. However, as tempting as he was, she must focus on her friends.

She tucked her hair behind her ear. "Did you talk to the families who hired my friends?"

Max wanted to chuckle at how cute Vivian looked trying to deny the attraction between them. He would let her for now. But once they reached London, he would make it impossible for her to deny his love.

He strolled across the library and settled in the chair again. "Yes, I did. I have guaranteed your friends' positions. The only reason they will face termination is if they disobey the terms of their employment."

Vivian felt a wave of relief. "You have my undying gratitude."

Max waved his hand in the air. "It was the least I could do. However, there is an issue regarding your friend Miss Grant."

Vivian's eyebrows drew together in confusion. "Regarding?"

"No one at the club is familiar with her employer. However, I learned the household she resides in is waiting for the new heir to arrive. Since I couldn't secure an arrangement with the lord, I have made other arrangements for Miss Flora Grant. Lord Lockhart and Lord Somerville have promised to look after her welfare. In the case the heir never arrives, they have promised her a position in their households. Or else they will send word so I can handle her situation," Max explained.

Vivian rose from the settee, untangling herself from the blanket. "Thank you so much. I am forever in your debt. Do you mind if I visit my friends this afternoon? I promise to finish the children's lessons before I go."

Max shook his head. "No."

"But ..."

"You can send word to meet them tomorrow morning before we leave for London. You need to stay here today to oversee the leave."

Vivian couldn't refuse his orders. Especially not after he had secured her friends' protection. She must obey his wishes and follow the path destined for her. If she wanted to keep earning wages to support her family, then she must abide by Max's demands. She would write to her friends and have Bowers send a footman to deliver her notes. If she hurried, she could write the missives before the children rose for breakfast.

Vivian nodded. "If you will please excuse me, I need to change before the children arise."

She tried to rush past him, but he caught her hand in his. "Vivian?"

Vivian paused and stared at their joined hands. She raised her gaze to Max, waiting for him to speak. However, he never spoke a word. He remained too much of a coward to express his emotions. So he stayed silent, dropping her hand. "'Tis nothing."

Vivian nodded before she left the library. She'd noted the emotions swirling in his gaze and had been too afraid to question him. She didn't want to learn of her dismissal once they reached London. Nor did she want to hope he would declare his love. If he loved her, then why not declare his feelings? Because he never did. She must accept she benefited his needs while he worked through his grief, a vessel to channel his emotions through.

She meant nothing more to him.

Chapter Twenty-One

V IVIAN WAITED ON THE bench for her friends to join her, watching the children chase each other around. Max waited for them near the carriage. He had agreed to let the children play since they would find themselves confined in the carriage over the next few days.

"Vivian!" Sara cried out, waving at her.

Vivian stood and wrapped Sara in a hug. She would miss her friends. She didn't know when she'd see them again. After they settled back on the bench, Flora and Grace joined them.

"I am sorry." The girls apologized at once.

"None of you need to apologize. 'Tis my fault for placing each of you in this situation. However, I have secured your positions. Lord Courtland has promised to help you find positions if something troublesome happens in your current employment."

"Ah, the knight in shining armor has ridden to rescue the damsel in distress and her friends," Grace said with a wink.

Vivian blushed. "I would not describe Lord Courtland in those terms."

"Then how else would you describe him? Your blush states otherwise," Flora teased.

"Umm ... That is ... He ..." Vivian stammered.

Sara shook her head at Grace and Flora. "Stop your teasing. Now tell us your news."

"I am returning to London with Lord Courtland and the children. We leave immediately. He allowed me to visit with you to explain how he secured your positions. Everyone but you, Flora."

Flora's lips pinched with disappointment. "I understand."

Vivian reached out to gather Flora's hands in hers. "However, Lord Lockhart and Lord Somerville have promised to speak to your employer once he arrives. If they cannot convince him to keep you employed, then they promised to find a position for you in their households or secure you another governess position. Have you heard any more of your mysterious employer?"

Flora shook her head. "No. Only the same rumor about how my employer inherited the title and needs a governess for his offspring. No one knows his identity or where he hails from."

"Once you discover, send word to Lord Lockhart or Lord Somerville. They will know how to contact Lord Courtland."

"And you, Vivian? What does your future hold? Is he Lord Courtland or Max to you?" Grace asked.

Vivian's gaze drifted to the carriage where Max stood outside of it, conversing with two gentlemen. "I am unsure. I would love to share how he has declared his love. However, I believe I've only served a purpose he will no longer need once we reach London."

Flora squeezed her hands in support. "Perhaps he waits until you return to London to profess his undying devotion."

Vivian swiped at the tear before it hit her cheek. "Perhaps but doubtful." She attempted to smile at her friends. "I will write to you once I find another position. Now please, before I leave, please promise you will stay in touch."

"We promise," Sara stated.

They stood and exchanged hugs. They promised to keep in touch with Vivian and look out for one another. While she had secured their positions and they had forgiven her, Vivian felt a profound sense of loss as she gathered the children to leave. It was as if a shift rippled through their bonds of friendship, dividing them for a spell.

Max shook Lockhart's and Somerville's hands. "Thank you for your help in this matter. I appreciate you watching over Miss Wescott's friends."

Somerville nodded. "It is the least we can do. Someone needs to offer them protection from a threat that is a foolish attempt at revenge."

Lockhart watched the group of young women. "I need to make you aware of a rumor I overheard at the club. The news of the girls' actions has reached Scotland. It is quite a scandalous tale that involves false accusations of how each girl presented themselves as a governess when they were actually the lord of the manor's mistress."

Max's face took on a thunderous expression. "Those are complete lies."

"I agree. However, it does not stop the slander from being spread. Once you reach London, you must find the source of these false accusations and make them regret uttering them. In the meantime, we will protect the ladies. I thought to warn you, so you can protect Miss Wescott on your return," Lockhart informed Max.

Max growled. "They will regret every slanderous lie that passed through their lips. Of that I promise you."

Somerville tilted his head toward Vivian and the children, who were drawing closer. "Have a safe journey."

Max fought to control his anger before Vivian reached them. "I will be in touch."

The gentlemen walked away, and Max turned around, pretending indifference at the conversation he just held. He wanted to rage at the injustices that awaited Vivian on her return to London. He debated if they should make a stop in Gretna Green and marry. Then no one would dare whisper the lies spreading about her. He would protect Vivian and her family with his name and his family's rank in society.

His reaction to protecting Vivian made him scoff at the irony of the situation. He'd always been too proud and strived to live his life with no scandal attached to his family. Now he wanted to marry Vivian to keep any scandal unattached to her, therefore allowing Max to carry the shame of the rumor under his name. If his reaction wasn't because of how deeply he loved Vivian, then he didn't know how else to describe the reason behind his thoughts.

However, he refused to marry Vivian because he wished to avoid scandal. Max wanted them to declare their love for one another and wed without a single whisper of gossip hanging over their heads. If he convinced her to elope, then she would always wonder if he truly loved her. He wanted no sense of obligation in their marriage bed. He held other plans on how to spend a lifetime with her. No. They would weather this scandal and expose the villain who had spread their lies of vindictiveness.

He smiled. "Did you have a friendly visit with your friends?"

"Yes. Lord Lockhart's brothers are swell," Bennett exclaimed.

"Lord Somerville's daughter said to bring my doll next time." Leah beamed.

Max chuckled at how the children responded to the question he'd meant for Vivian. "Perhaps on our return, Miss Wescott can arrange for the children to visit your home and you can entertain them in the nursery."

The children expressed their glee with excited chatter as Max helped them into the carriage. He noticed the surprised look on Vivian's face, and he never elaborated. He just kept her wondering about where her future lay. It wasn't fair of him, but he needed to keep her unsure of his plans for them to work to his advantage.

Max held out his hand to help Vivian board the carriage. "And your visit?"

A tingling sensation coursed through Vivian when she placed her fingers in his hand. The journey would be a torturous ordeal spending time with Max in such intimate quarters, even with the children between them. She didn't know whether to feel relieved that he stated she still held a position as the children's governess or saddened because they held no future. He crushed her hopes but also gave her the security that he wouldn't abandon her once she arrived in London. She could still help her family and protect her sister's welfare.

To desire otherwise was a selfish wish.

"It was pleasant. Thank you for allowing me to say my goodbyes before we left." Vivian settled on the seat next to Leah.

Max tilted his head. "My pleasure." He tapped the roof of the carriage, signaling for the driver to embark on the journey.

Vivian tried to ignore Max's intense gaze by seeing to the children's needs, but she failed when her gaze kept connecting with his. She didn't understand the hidden meaning behind his look. She tried to erect the walls around her heart with valid points on why she needed to protect herself from Max. But she failed. Vivian needed to face the facts that her fate lay at the mercy of Maximilian Courtland.

The lord who held her heart.

Chapter Twenty-Two

MAX STARED ACROSS THE carriage as the children drifted to sleep, cuddled into Vivian. The past few days of travel had only endeared Vivian to his heart with her gentle devotion toward the children. He now understood what she had tried to tell him when she first arrived in Scotland. Her message not only pertained to the children's loss but also to her own suffering. She held a special kinship with Bennett and Leah and always would. She would make a wonderful mother to his children.

"The children have taken quite well to you," Max whispered.

Vivian gazed down at the children with a smile gracing her lips. "I simply adore them."

"You will make a very loving mother," Max observed.

Vivian stiffened. "An act which will never come to fruition."

Max realized he had ventured into dangerous territory with this conversation, but he couldn't resist. They would reach London this evening, and he hoped Vivian would show him a sign that she cared about him.

"I hold a different opinion. Why do you believe it will not come true?"

"Perhaps because I no longer hold a position where I can make wishes over silly infatuations," Vivian answered with sarcasm tinging her words.

Max smiled. "Perhaps it is because you no longer hold faith in your wishes."

Vivian looked out the window, biting the inside of her cheek. She wanted to rail at Max for his insensitive nature in discussing such an intimate subject of impossibility. However, she refused to show him how the topic affected her.

She turned her gaze back to stare at him and arched her eyebrow. "No, my lord. It is because I have accepted the path I now travel upon and understand the realistic guidelines I must live my life by now."

Max nodded. "Perhaps 'tis the wrong path you have taken your journey on. Perhaps another path will lead you to your destination."

Vivian scoffed. "There are too many perhaps in your observation than what is the truth."

Max's smile displayed the same wickedness shining from his gaze. "Perhaps."

Before Vivian responded to him, he reached over to lift Bennett and cushion him in the spot next to him. This allowed Vivian to slide over and allow Leah to lie across her lap. Max handed Vivian a blanket, and she covered the child while Max covered Bennett.

Vivian watched Max as he murmured to Bennett to make him more comfortable. She should return the compliment to him, but she couldn't bring herself to utter the words. He would make an excellent father. Especially once he found the perfect caring wife. She only hoped the lady embraced Bennett and Leah as her own, the way Max had. She no longer worried about their care.

Once they reached London, she would take it upon herself to find another governess for the children. As much as she loved them, her heart refused to endure watching Max fall in love with another woman and making her his wife.

A position she craved for herself.

Once they arrived in London, Vivian settled the children into a routine, oblivious to the rumors circulating the ton's gossip mill. Max searched endlessly for the culprit but to no avail. It was an impossible feat. It wouldn't take long before Vivian learned of the slander. So far, he had kept the rumor from reaching her ears. But with Joy's wedding tomorrow and her insistence on Vivian's attendance, the ugliness would surface.

He managed to keep the news of Vivian's return from her family, but once they saw her at the wedding, all hell would break loose. Her sorry excuse of a family believed the rumors and had sworn to everyone that they had disowned her. All except her sister. However, Chloe hadn't reached an age where she could separate herself from her family.

Disgust at their reaction kept him from his promise to repair their fractured state of survival. Before his return, he had decided to pay off her family's debt and encourage other prominent families to accept them back into their fold. However, now he only wanted to sink their demise further into existence.

Now he must either tell Vivian about the false accusations or deny her access to attend Joy's wedding with an excuse. Max didn't want to act the brute, but he must protect her. He could handle Vivian's anger and Joy's disappointment if it kept Vivian from being shamed. He would inform her that he had changed his mind about the children attending the ceremony and force her to remain at his residence to care for them, then never return for them for the breakfast reception. Once he returned home, the celebration would be over. Yes. It was an excellent plan. However, plans never progressed the way one wanted them to.

He followed the sound of the children's voices and found Vivian visiting with Joy in the library. Bennett and Leah regaled Joy about the new friends they had made back home. Damn. His sister's arrival ruined his plans. Why was she here? Shouldn't her wedding plans keep her overwhelmed?

Joy caught his gaze and tilted her head to Vivian, and he gave a discreet shake of his head. She shook her head in disapproval and mouthed, "Why?" Max shrugged. His only excuse was to protect Vivian until the rumor mill found a juicier bit of gossip. However, the ton found this rumor too scintillating to surrender their interest.

Max brushed a kiss across his sister's cheek. "Should you not be scurrying around with your wedding plans?"

"Scurrying around? You make me sound like a rodent." Joy acted affronted.

"Like a rat." Bennett laughed.

"No. Like a rabbit," Leah added.

"Well, a rabbit sounds lovely." Joy tapped Leah on the nose. "But a rat?" Joy shuddered. "No, thank you."

Leah started hopping around the parlor like a rabbit, and soon Bennett followed her lead. Joy laughed at their antics. "It is good to hear their laughter."

"A result of Vivian's care," Max complimented.

Vivian blushed. "I cannot take all the credit. They flourish from the time you spend with them."

Joy glanced back and forth between her brother and Vivian, amazed that animosity no longer lingered between them. It would seem the two had settled their differences after she left Scotland. And if Vivian's blush and the way her brother regarded her friend were anything to go by, then it would appear their relationship had taken an intimate turn. Joy only hoped Max didn't let Vivian slip through his fingers again.

Joy smiled at her brother. "Max, would you be a dear and take the children outside to play in the gardens? I need to speak with Vivian about the wedding."

Max stepped forward. "If you will allow me ..."

Joy held her hand up to stop her brother from lying. A lie that would hurt his chances with Vivian. "No. You had your chance."

Vivian's head swiveled back and forth as Max and Joy appeared to have a silent argument concerning her wedding. An uneasy sensation coursed through Vivian that they needed to tell her something unpleasant. Something Max should've warned her about but hadn't. Did it concern the mishap she had caused with Lord Baldridge? Surely, that debacle had fallen out of favor for another titillating piece of gossip by now.

"Fine," Max growled. "Children, follow me." Max guided the children out of the French doors that led to the garden.

Joy waited for the children to lead Max deeper into the gardens before she turned toward Vivian. It broke her heart to inform her friend of the ton's cruel rumor, and she cursed her brother for being a coward and not confronting the issue.

"What is wrong?" Vivian asked.

Joy sighed. "There is a rumor circulating across London about you and your governess friends."

Vivian tensed. Joy's serious expression meant there was more being said than what actually happened. An even more dire offense than the letter she had received. Whatever it was, it meant to destroy her.

Vivian gripped her hands together. "What slanderous accusations is the ton whispering about?"

Joy took a deep breath. "That your positions as governesses were only a front and your actual positions were mistresses to the lords who employed you."

Vivian paled at the accusation, never expecting something so terrible to be said about her. She collapsed back against the cushions. The horror of the slander kept her from responding. A charge of this claim would damage her family and every family involved. This would ruin her sister's chances of ever gaining an offer from a proper prospect.

Her hands trembled as she covered her face. "Does Max know?"

"Yes," Joy whispered.

Of course, he knew. It surprised Vivian that he hadn't thrown her out. If anyone in the ton learned she worked for him as a governess, then it would bring about scandal to his pristine family name. Was this the reason he had insisted that they recover from their journey before Vivian took the children around London? The shame she caused him and the children brought a wave of heartache. She wanted to laugh at the irony of the rumor. However, there was no humor behind the truth. It was how she now earned her coin with Max.

She leapt from the settee and rushed toward her bedchamber. Joy kept calling after her, and Vivian quickened her pace. Once she reached the bedchamber, she started throwing her belongings onto the bed to pack. If she hurried, she could avoid Max and the children before they came back inside.

Vivian spun around, looking for anything she might've missed. A vast pile lay on the bed in her desperation to leave as swiftly as possible. She choked back a cry at the security she felt slipping from her fingers.

A pair of hands grabbed her, turning her around. Max wrapped her in his embrace and held her tight against him. "Shh, love. I've got you."

Vivian thrashed her head back and forth against Max's chest. "You must let me go. You cannot allow a servant to see you in my bedchamber. It will ruin you."

"To hell with the servants," Max growled.

"I must leave." Vivian tried to break Max's hold.

"You are going nowhere."

Tears streamed down Vivian's cheeks. "You must consider the children."

Max pulled back far enough to make his point clear to Vivian. "I am. They need you. They have already lost the most important people in their lives. I will not allow the petty opinions of others to destroy their sense of family."

"Then consider your family's reputation you have fought so hard to maintain," Vivian argued.

Max ran his hand along Vivian's hair in tender affection. "None of that matters anymore."

"It must."

Max shook his head in denial. Before he could declare his love for Vivian, Joy knocked on the door, interrupting them. "May I come in?"

Max dropped his arms and stepped back from Vivian. "Yes. Will you please help Vivian put away her belongings? I must see to a matter of importance."

Max stalked from the bedchamber before Vivian could continue her argument to leave. She stared at Joy helplessly, unsure what to do. Joy held out her arms to Vivian, and she fell into them, crying out her sorrow. Joy guided them to the divan and held Vivian until she fell into an exhausted slumber.

After Vivian fell asleep, Joy covered her with a blanket. Then she hung Vivian's dresses in the wardrobe and put her other belongings away. She closed the door and made her way to her brother's study. Joy found Max pacing back and forth across the rug.

"You cannot lose her again," Joy declared.

"I have no intention to," Max growled.

Joy nodded, satisfied with Max's passionate response. However, her curiosity about Max's and Vivian's change of behavior had yet to be appeased. It was only a few months back that she had found her brother acting in the same manner after he broke off his betrothal with Vivian. He never explained his reason then, but Joy would no longer stand for his silence.

She settled into an armchair. "I am curious, dear brother. Why the reverse acceptance of Vivian in your life?"

Max stopped his pacing to glare at his sister. When he noted her relaxed pose, he realized she wouldn't leave until he explained himself. He hadn't wanted to bother her with the drama when she should be celebrating the happiest moment of her life. However, Joy cared for Vivian as much as he did, and he needed her to help him convince Vivian of his love. Especially since he had ruined their relationship by not trusting her.

Max thrust his fingers through his hair. "Because I was a fool who allowed myself to believe a trusted peer instead of believing in Vivian's love."

Joy pointed at the chair across from her for Max to sit. "Explain yourself."

Max sat down, running his hands along the chair's arms. "When Vivian's family fell from grace, I had my doubts about our union. While part of me wanted to protect her, I allowed my pride to stand in the way of keeping scandal from becoming attached to our family name."

"Oh, Maximilian. Do not tell me that is the reason you broke the betrothal? If so, then you do not deserve Vivian's love ever. Not then and certainly not now."

Max turned his head, unable to meet his sister's gaze. "I considered it the reason to break from her. But it was not the ultimate reason for my decision."

"Then what was?"

"I was at my club, drinking my sorrows away at the decision I needed to make when I overheard Lord Packwood brag of a conquest he had secured after several attempts at seduction. He was very explicit about the details of the debutante he ruined. And when I couldn't feel more despondent, Packwood sauntered over to me and thanked me for throwing Vivian over. Because it made his evening a success."

Max paused, staring up at the ceiling. "His comment confirmed my suspicions that Vivian had attached herself to me for financial gain for her family. Vivian went and found herself another benefactor to become her husband when I ignored her after her father's scandal."

Joy shook her head in distress. "No!"

Max swung his haunted gaze back to his sister. "I realize that now. However, at the time, I believed Packwood's story. I left the club to confront Vivian. I remember the look of relief in her eyes when she saw me. I took her excitement as a sign. She felt relieved she didn't lose her chance to sink her claws into me. In my anger, I set out to destroy her like she had me."

Joy's eyes filled with tears. "What did you say to her?"

Max leapt from the chair to pace again. "Everything deplorable you can imagine. I tore her character to shreds, calling her a fortune-hunter whore who used her body to her advantage. Then I questioned why she never spread her legs for me since she wanted to secure herself financial security. Among other slanderous words I am not proud to admit to."

Joy covered her hand over her mouth. "Oh my goodness. Tell me this is all a lie."

Max never refuted his comments. His silence spoke of his guilt. That same guilt settled in his gut, festering and prodding him with the sickness of the actions he had committed to someone he had sworn to love. He didn't deserve Vivian's love from his behavior alone. However, he was a selfish bastard who refused to abandon her again.

"Do you still believe Lord Packwood spoke the truth?" Joy asked.

"Every single bloody word out of his mouth was a lie." Max scoffed. "All damn lies."

"Since you did not believe in Vivian's innocence before, why do you now?"

"Because I ..." Max stopped. He turned away from Joy and swore. He'd almost told his sister how he had learned the truth.

Joy gasped. "You ruined Vivian." She tugged on his arm, trying to swing him around. When he wouldn't turn, Joy stomped around him to witness the guilty expression on his face. "Do you realize what you have done?"

"I am well aware of the consequences of my actions and how they affect Vivian."

Joy thumped him on the chest. "The very rumors spreading about her amongst the ton now hold true because of the position you placed her in. I cannot believe your insensitivity. Is this how you sought revenge for your battered pride?"

Max strode to pour himself a drink. He threw back the shot of whiskey in one gulp and then poured himself another. "You misunderstand. I never intended to hurt Vivian. I held no clue about the lies spreading about how she gained employment. Lord Lockhart informed me of the rumors before we left Scotland, and by then, it was too late. We had already committed the act. An act I will not regret, mind you. I love Vivian. No matter how difficult it will be, I will prove my love to her. She will become my bride, and we will create a family together. On that, I swear to you."

No lies would come between them ever again.

Chapter Twenty-Three

V IVIAN BIT AT HER lip to keep her cry of anguish from pouring out. She had never understood the accusations Max flung at her when he broke off their betrothal, only what they implicated. He had refused to listen to her side of the story, branding her a money-hungry harlot. She thought Lord Packwood had bragged about the kiss he'd forced upon her. Never did she imagine he had lied to Max about bedding her. She'd slapped him and called him a gutter swine toad. She should've known that with the way she'd stung Packwood's pride, he would strike out with his retaliation. But never to the degree he did.

She picked up her valise and left Max's home with what remained of her pride. She couldn't bear to listen to any more. However, her footsteps led her away before she heard his declaration.

To protect Max and the children, she must return home to her family. A broken mess, but her only option. Her friends were too far away to offer her a shoulder to cry on. At least they weren't subjected to the degrading rumors. Max's offer to protect them was a blessing in disguise.

Vivian slipped out of the servants' entrance and continued along the alleyway to her parents' townhome. Once she reached the townhome, she saw the disrepair already taking shape in the garden. With limited funds, her parents had dismissed the servants, only retaining enough to keep the house running. They misled the ton with the pretense that they hadn't fallen on hard times.

She trudged up the stairs and set the valise on her bed before she opened the adjoining door to her sister's bedchamber. She peeked her head inside and saw her sister reading a book on the chaise near the window. Vivian smiled at how Chloe hadn't noticed her yet. She loved her sister dearly, and the shame she must suffer from the fact they were sisters broke her heart.

Before she surprised Chloe, her mother flung the door open to Chloe's bedchamber and stormed inside. "How dare you show your face under this roof! Do you not have a care about how you've ruined your sister's good name?"

Vivian should've expected a hurtful response to her return. Her mother had used a shrill tone toward her on more than one occasion. Especially when her behavior reflected poorly on her sister. She had never once taken Vivian's feelings into account. Her mother had never cared about the truth, only about how others would perceive her.

Once upon a time, Vivian had been the favorite daughter while Max courted her. When he proposed, her mother had doted on her. However, once Max broke the betrothal, her mother had treated her worse than a distant relative. Instead, her mother focused her attention on Chloe. She attempted to lure an unsuspecting gentleman into their trap of gaining financial wealth for their family, whether or not Chloe loved her prospected groom.

"Mama," Chloe shrieked. She ran across the room and threw herself into Vivian's arms. "Vivian, you have come home."

Vivian hugged her sister. She wanted to cry her sorrows and have someone she loved offer her comfort. Not argue with her mother and guard her sister against their mother's wrath. The haughty glare from her mother showed she wished for the impossible. It was foolish of her to imagine her family would offer their protection when they never had in the past. In her desperation, she'd considered them her only option. However, Vivian would gain no support in this household. She must leave if she wanted the scandal to remain unattached to her sister's name.

"Gather your valise, and Waters will see you out," her mother informed her. Lady Wescott turned to the footman. "Make sure she departs from the servants' entrance. We cannot risk our reputation and anyone witnessing her presence in this household."

"You cannot turn Vivian away. She needs us now more than ever," Chloe argued.

"I can and I will. Your sister has brought nothing but disgrace to our family's name. If anyone were to learn of her return, they would slam every door in our faces. Do you want Lord Heybrook to withdraw his courtship? Because if you attach yourself to your sister, then you'll need to find yourself a position as a servant, too."

"Mother is correct." Vivian peeled herself away from Chloe. "I only wanted to check on your welfare and visit for a spell. I did not mean to cause any discord with your future happiness."

Vivian knew better than to plead her case to her mother or go belowstairs to cry to her father. They were two immovable forces who only acted in their best interest, not those of their children. Nor could she ask her brothers for help because they were as selfish as her parents.

She only had two options. Return to Max or find lodging for the evening and make plans for her future. She hurried back to her bedchamber and gathered her valise. She looked over her shoulder at Chloe, who had tears streaming down her face. Vivian attempted a smile but failed miserably.

However, she tilted her chin high when she walked by her mother. "Good day, Lady Wescott."

Her mother gasped at her audacity, and that brought a genuine smile to Vivian's lips.

As she stood in the alleyway, she glanced longingly back toward Max's townhome. Instead of walking in his direction, she turned the opposite way and walked until she came upon a street. She hired a hackney with instructions to find her an inn on the outskirts of London. No one would search for her there. She would spend the evening devising a new plan for the next step of her journey.

Perhaps even cry a tear or two.

Max sat in the church's pew, watching his sister marry his best mate. He was beyond thrilled about their union but miserable at the same time. When they spoke their vows, it made the entire fiasco with Vivian even more unbearable. He wanted to roar at every guest present, at the injustice they had handed Vivian because of their own spitefulness. But he wouldn't ruin his sister's wedding. Already, a cloud hung over the festivities at Vivian's disappearance.

She'd left no clue of where to find her. He'd stormed over to her parents' home, only for Lady Wescott to yammer on about how disgraceful she found Vivian's behavior, that Vivian was no longer welcome in their home and they had disowned her. Then she had the audacity to tell him that he should feel thankful he didn't find himself saddled with Vivian for a wife. Especially since she was so free with her favors.

He'd left there more outraged for Vivian than when he'd arrived. At least her sister had caught him before he left and informed him that Vivian had come home, but her mother had ordered her to leave. Chloe had no clue where Vivian had disappeared to. Max had scoured the surrounding area for any sign of her, questioning neighbors if they'd seen her. But at the first mention of her name, everyone denied any association and refused to talk to him.

Max had to attend the breakfast reception and see to the children's welfare before he continued his search for Vivian. He swore to Chloe and Joy that he would find her.

He glanced at the children sitting next to him, acting with the best of manners. Vivian would be so proud of them. Hell! He was proud of their behavior. While they were still heathens who hooped and hollered like Scottish warriors, they were also two well-behaved children. And all because of Vivian's love and guidance. Yes. She would make an excellent mother to their children. Now he only needed to find her and convince her of his love.

He smiled at how Bennett kept tugging on his cravat and swinging his legs back and forth on the pew, while Leah sat there in awe of the wedding nuptials. Even though the little girl loved stories of pirate treasures, she also fancied herself a princess.

A tingling sensation tickled his neck. He glanced over his shoulder to scan the church, looking for anyone who might stare at him. However, everyone's gaze stayed fastened on the groom kissing his bride. The guests clapped when Bradley pulled away from Joy. Max stood and clapped as his sister and her husband walked down the aisle. He hung back with the children while everyone offered their well-wishes. When the church cleared out, he ushered the children to the carriage waiting to take them to his parents' home, where his mother had a huge celebration planned.

Vivian stared at Max from the balcony of the church. He looked splendid in his suit coat, with his cravat matching the color of his eyes. She couldn't take her eyes off him.

She attended the wedding because she had promised Joy she would. While many unsavory comments were whispered about Vivian's character, she never broke a promise. However, she never watched one minute of the ceremony. As soon as Max walked into the church and settled the children next to him, he captured her attention.

Vivian had spent a restless night tossing and turning in bed until she decided she couldn't care less what anyone said about her. Max's opinion was the only one that mattered. And until she braved the unknown and told him she loved him, she couldn't decide the path of her journey. Vivian loved him with all her heart, and she believed Max loved her too. Before, his accusations had shocked her, and she'd walked away without fighting for him. However, after enduring the past year by only relying on herself, she decided she would fight to the ends of the earth for Max's love.

When he turned around, searching amongst the guests, she thought he might've spotted her tucked in the corner. He even lingered behind after everyone, as if he waited for her to join him. However, she remained a coward and stayed hidden. She didn't want to ruin Joy's special day and would wait until the celebration concluded before she professed her feelings. She smiled at how well Max took care of the children as if they were his own.

Yes. He would make an excellent father to their children.

Chapter Twenty-Four

False Rumors

M AX CHECKED ON THE children to see if they slept peacefully before
he continued to his bedchamber. He stopped outside the room
Vivian had used, resting his hand on the frame. He worried about her and
wondered where she kept herself hidden. Max wished he could share the
news of the latest rumors floating around the ton, the kind of rumor that
painted her and her friends in a different light. He had yet to discover who
had tarnished her name with such venom, but he swore he wouldn't rest until
he did. In the meantime, his friends had helped support his love for Vivian
by spreading a fresh set of rumors, making her character shine.

Even Vivian's mother attempted to redeem herself. However, he gave her
the cut direct and turned his back on her in mid-sentence. He heard her
sputtering behind him and smiled a victory at his success in putting the
lady in her place. Vivian might find disappointment with him, but it was
a declaration of how he planned to protect her for the rest of her life. Even
from someone as close to her as her own mother.

Max walked into his bedchamber, discarding his cravat and suit coat. He
unbuttoned his vest and was almost finished disrobing when he caught

movement out of the corner of his eye. He turned and found Vivian curled up in his armchair near the fire. Her head rested against the armchair cushions.

He almost dropped to his knees at the relief of seeing her safely within his grasp. Max's eyes drank her in. Her hair rested around her shoulders in waves, and she wore a simple dress. His gaze traveled the length of her body. Her dress had ridden up her legs, displaying her long limbs for his perusal. They lay bare, her stockings discarded on the floor with her slippers. Hope flared through him at her appearance.

Hope but most of all love.

He sat on the ottoman in front of the chair, admiring the sight of her and soaking in what her appearance might mean. He wouldn't need to comb London in an impossible feat to locate her. At this moment, he didn't know if he should wake her. The darkness under her eyes urged him to let her rest. They had plenty of time when she awakened to discuss their situation.

Max stood and pulled the blanket back on his bed. He lifted Vivian into his arms and laid her on the mattress. After discarding his boots and pulling off his shirt, he slid in next to Vivian. She didn't so much as stir but sighed as Max pulled her into his arms. She'd never felt more heavenly than she did now.

He lost count of how many times the clock chimed the next hour as he stared at Vivian, asleep in his arms. Each light snore, incoherent mumble, and sigh as she snuggled against him lightened his heart and brought forth a permanent smile to his lips. Oh, he understood what awaited them outside his bedchamber. He wasn't a fool to believe any rumor that spread about their union would be hurtful to Vivian. But at least he no longer had to worry about her. He would protect her from the harm of evildoers, and together they would fight through this storm and come out victorious.

Vivian's eyelids fluttered before opening wide in shock. She stiffened against him, her fingers clenching into a fist against his stomach. How Max kept his breathing even as she realized her surroundings amazed even him. Her gaze darted around before it landed on him.

"Max?" Her husky whisper echoed around them.

Max ran his hand along her hair, gently stroking her to remain calm. "Yes, my love?"

Max chuckled as Vivian's face turned a fiery red. She pushed against him, trying to rise, but Max only tightened his hold. Now that he held her in his arms, he refused to let her go again.

"I never meant ... I only wanted ..." Vivian stammered.

With Max holding her, Vivian grew flustered from explaining why she was in his bedchamber. It was the only place she would have his full attention, with no one catching sight of her. She had hidden in the room they gave her when she overheard Max telling his valet to take the evening off. Then she had snuck into his room and waited for him to return from Joy's wedding celebration.

Max tipped her chin up and lowered his head. He took her mouth under his in an achingly sweet kiss that had her softening against him. He traced his tongue across her lips with one slow swipe after another, and she sighed, opening her mouth. Still, he never rushed, stroking his tongue against hers in a dance as slow as time.

"Max." Vivian sighed.

Her sigh was his undoing. He pulled her across his chest, combing his fingers through her hair as he ravished her lips with one kiss after another. Savoring the taste of her was an exquisite rush of satisfaction. He trailed a path of kisses down her neck and along her silky skin as he unbuttoned her dress. He should stop and profess his love before he continued, but the thrill of Vivian in his arms kept him from acting in any rational manner.

Vivian had lost herself to Max's seduction the second she awoke in his embrace. With each kiss and caress from his fingertips, her body rose to a new high, and she never wanted to have her feet touch the ground. She should ask him to stop until she confessed her love, but her heart refused to give him the chance to rebuff her. No. She wanted to capture another memory to keep her warm on the lonely nights soon to come.

Her hands spread across his bare chest, and his heat seared straight to her soul. She traced her fingers with slow precision across the hard ridges, stroking the muscles that cushioned her body. She pressed her lips against his warm skin in a light kiss, so light she thought he might not feel it. However, his body tensed at the slight gesture. When she licked the path her fingers traveled, he tightened the grip on her hair, holding her head to his chest.

With a smile at the effect she held over him, Vivian trailed her kisses lower. The lower she drifted, the hotter the flames of desire licked the path along with her. She shifted her body, and his cock pressed against her breasts. Vivian tore at the buttons on the placket of his trousers, eager to hold Max's throbbing desire in her hand.

Vivian squeezed her thighs together as her fingers wrapped around Max's cock. She ached to have him slide inside her and make them one. However, she desired to pleasure him even more. To hear his moans reflect the passion swirling around them. Her hand glided down the length of his cock in the slowest of strokes with each hiss of his breath, drawing out a plea for her to satisfy him.

She raised her head, peeking out from her lowered lids at the ecstasy crossing his features. Vivian froze from the passion swirling inside Max's gaze. He didn't hide the love he felt for her. With renewed focus, she twirled her tongue around the tip before wrapping her lips and sucking softly. Her tongue pressed against the steady beat of his need while she guided him into her mouth.

"Christ, Vivian," Max growled, wrapping his fingers in her hair and tightening his grip.

Max drowned at the exhilarating sensation of Vivian's lips gliding down his cock, drawing him deeper into her mouth to the back of her throat. She was relentless at sending him spiraling over the abyss with each delicious lick of his flesh. When she hummed her enjoyment, it sent a thrill coursing through his veins to claim her and possess her with all his heart and desire.

Vivian slid Max out of her mouth to draw a breath before she devoured him again. However, before she lowered her mouth around his cock, he pulled her up his body, sank his teeth into her bottom lip, and sucked it inside his mouth. His tongue invaded her mouth, exploring every surface and attacking her senses with his relentless pursuit of the unknown.

He rolled them over, rose above Vivian, and ripped her dress down the middle. "I'll buy you a dozen more," Max growled, pulling it away from her body.

Her chemise experienced the same treatment at his hands, leaving Vivian too breathless with desire to complain otherwise. The desperation she suffered from wondering if Max ever loved her disappeared. A whimper escaped her when Max cupped her breasts and tugged on her nipples. A sigh followed as his tongue caressed the buds with languid strokes.

"Oh my," Vivian moaned.

Vivian's leg rose along his and hooked around his waist as he suckled on her nipples, drawing them into hardened buds between his lips. Her wet core brushed across his aching cock. He bit down on a nipple, and her nails dug into his arm. Her moans played a melody around them as he sought his pleasure with her delectable form.

He snaked a hand between their bodies and sank his fingers into her wetness, drawing them through her folds before sliding a finger deep inside her. He rubbed his thumb across her clit, strumming until she raised her hips and pressed into his touch, seeking her relief. However, he wanted to string her need to a height where only his cock would give her the relief she craved. With another finger, he stroked her body into a dance, searching for its partner.

"Max, please," Vivian begged.

Max scraped his teeth across her sensitive bud. "Please what, sweet Vivian?"

Max tormented Vivian and teased her body, bringing her to the brink, only to slow his caresses and leave her begging. Her head thrashed against the pillow as her body ached to find the sweet oblivion only Max could gift her. He left her unable to breathe her demands with the strum of his fingers, drawing out her desires to his satisfaction.

He lifted his fingers from her core and drew each one inside his mouth, sucking on the delicious flavor of her desire. Vivian's gaze clung to his display of erotic behavior. "While I would love to bury my head between your thighs and suck every succulent drop of dew from your pussy, I cannot wait another minute to claim you as mine."

Before the last hypnotizing word floated to her ears, he filled her with his cock, sinking into the heaven her body craved. Vivian arched into him, clinging to him as he dominated her senses with a need so powerful it left them both quaking from the torrents of emotions coursing through them, molding them into one.

"Stay with me …" Max demanded. His request held more meaning than their act of making love. It signified that he couldn't live another day without her beside him. "Forever."

Max bent his head and kissed Vivian with such tenderness, a fresh wave of tears streamed along her cheeks. The drops mingled on their tongues as their bodies forged together as one.

Each movement sent their passion climbing to a height impossible for them to scale, yet together they reached the pinnacle before flying over the ledge of heartache and soaring into the open wind of forgiveness. Max wrapped Vivian in his embrace as they collapsed against the pillows.

Her tears still fell, splashing on his chest. There were no words to ease her distress. The harsh reality of what had befallen her and her family's reaction was something they would accept together and move forward and hopefully, in time, repair. If not, then they would find comfort in the family they created.

For now, Max held Vivian and gave her the security he never should have stolen away from her. And he offered her the love she had always held but he'd kept from her while he was a fool.

A mistake he would never make again.

Chapter Twenty-Five

VIVIAN TOOK A DEEP breath and wiped the tears off her cheeks. It was time to confront Max about the troubles she must face. She could no longer avoid the inevitable.

"May we talk?" Vivian asked.

Max tightened his hold, afraid Vivian would flee again. "Yes."

Vivian pressed her hand against his chest. "Will you please let me go, then?"

"Never."

Vivian raised her head and smiled at Max's defiance. "I promise not to run."

"I am not giving you a chance to."

"Please. I wish to have this conversation with no temptation."

Max smirked. "Do you find me tempting?"

Vivian rolled her eyes. "About as tempting as you find me."

"Mmm," Max murmured before dipping his head to steal a kiss. "Miss Westcott, I find you beyond tempting."

Vivian dropped her gaze. "Miss Westcott?" She pushed out of his hold, wrapping the blanket around her.

"Damn," Max growled. "I was only teasing you, Vivian."

Max yanked on his trousers, rushing around the bed. He grabbed Vivian by the shoulders to keep her in place and tilted her chin to stare into the outrage blazing from her eyes. He kept making a muck out of apologizing to her, offending her at every turn. Max dropped his hold and stood back. He scooped his shirt off the floor and drew it over Vivian's head. Her arms poked through the sleeves, and she attempted to pull it past her knees but failed.

Vivian wrapped her arms around herself, feeling even more vulnerable without Max holding her. She cursed her sensitivity regarding Max. However, his past treatment still stung her pride. Not to mention how it tore her feelings asunder. However, if they were to move forward, then she must forgive the past.

Vivian tucked her hair behind her ears. "Thank you."

Max nodded. He shoved his hands behind his back to keep himself from reaching for Vivian and returning her into his embrace. Vivian curled back into the armchair, and he waited for her to speak. When she remained quiet, staring into the fire, he moved to sit down and put her at ease.

Vivian swung her gaze back to him. "Why did you believe such a horrid lie about me? Did you not see how much I adored you?" Vivian continued, not allowing Max a chance to answer her. "You left me destitute with your rejection. I loved you, and it meant nothing to you."

"Loved me?"

Vivian narrowed her gaze. "No! You have no right to question how I may or may not care for you until you state the reasons for your behavior."

Max ran a hand down his face, collecting his thoughts on how to answer Vivian. No matter how much it made him look like an unfeeling bastard, Vivian deserved to hear the truth. "Because I had doubts about the love you professed once I learned of your family's demise. I overheard rumors of how your ambition was to secure a catch to save your family. Then, when Lord Packwood shared in detail how you cuckolded me before the ceremony even took place, I lost what love I held for you. My sense of pride demanded I end our relationship and secure my family from having any scandal attached to their name."

"You held no love for me to begin with," Vivian accused.

Max sat forward in his chair, reaching out to her. But Vivian only curled up more within herself. "Yes, I did."

Vivian shook her head. "No. Not in the way I needed."

Max hung his head in shame. "No. Not in the way you deserved."

"Thank you for being honest."

"I allowed my pride and my foolish sense of obligation to steal away my happiness. After we parted ways, every day of my existence I spent in misery. However, I kept denying the reason for my misery. It was because your smile no longer existed. The warmth of your hand no longer held firm in my hand. Your soft sighs when we kissed never sung in the air surrounding me."

Max's declaration held a bittersweet quality to her battered heart. "And now? I am scandal personified. My family has disowned me. I cannot depend on you to rescue me, yet I have nowhere to turn. To make matters worse, my heart still yearns with unbridled love and devotion for a gentleman I can never have."

Max swore his heart stopped beating for a fraction of a minute at her confession of loving him. He feared she would reject him. However, she gave him hope. "Is that so horrible?"

"What, my family's rejection or the love I hold for you?"

Max smiled. "The love you hold for me."

Vivian sniffed. "It would not matter if you returned those feelings in the same regard. Not out of pity but how your heart would wither and die if you did not share every day with me."

Max rose from his chair and knelt before her, drawing her hands into his. "Vivian, my love. Yes. The words slide off my tongue with ease because I love you with all my heart and soul. The love you deserve and the kind I will shower you with, if you pledge your heart to me the same."

Vivian cupped Max's cheeks. "Are you sure? It is not the attraction between us that urges you to speak these false declarations?"

Max rose and lifted Vivian onto his lap. He kissed her with tender affection, as if she were a fragile ornament he feared he would break. "I am irrevocably, madly in love with you, Lady Vivian, and I pledge not a single day will pass without me showing you."

"And the scandal I have brought to your door?"

"I will take pleasure in destroying the person who dared to utter the slander against your good name," Max growled.

"I refuse to ruin your reputation or make the children's lives unbearable by your connection to me. Before I left town, I wanted to declare my love to you," Vivian explained.

"You are going nowhere. Do you hear me?" Max declared.

Vivian's smile held sadness. "I must."

"No!" Max gritted out between his teeth.

Vivian soothed her thumb across his eyebrows, easing his tension away. "Max, be reasonable. We can be nothing more than lovers. As much as I love you, I cannot hide away and only share your bed and nothing more."

Max stole another kiss. "You will continue to share my bed. But as my wife. You will be a mother to Bennett and Leah and any children we are fortunate to have."

"But your good name?"

"To hell with my good name." Another kiss graced her lips. Then another and another until Max had stolen her every breath into silence. "Do you not understand? None of that matters to me anymore. Only you matter."

How could Vivian not believe him when she felt the depth of his love with each kiss? "And the rumors circulating amongst the ton?"

A cocky grin lit Max's face. "Rumors that are turning those false statements into lies as I hold you in my arms. I have yet to find the identity of the culprit who set out to destroy innocent girls' lives, but I promise you I will."

"How?"

"Through my network of friends, we are clearing you and your friends' names. I have sent word to Lord Lockhart and Lord Somerville in Scotland about stopping the threat. They will tell your friends, so they no longer need to worry. But you can reassure them upon our return."

Vivian's eyebrows drew together. "Our return?"

"Yes. I've decided the favorable setting for Bennett and Leah to grieve and accept the changes in their lives is to reside in Scotland for a while. And on the journey back to the estate, I hope I can convince you to enjoy a day in Gretna Green, where you become my bride. Unless you would like a wedding at St. James Church."

Vivian's eyes widened. "You wish to marry me?"

Max chuckled at her surprise. "I love you, Vivian. Will you do me the honor of becoming Lady Courtland? Please answer yes."

There was no other answer but yes. However, Vivian was too overcome with emotion to utter the simple word. She responded the only way she could. She drew Max's head to hers and gave him a kiss filled with her love.

The longer she didn't answer him, the more anxious Max became. But when she pulled him in for a kiss, all of Max's doubts vanished. He didn't need her to declare her love and devotion. Her kiss gave him the answer he wished for.

Max nestled Vivian against him, clasping their hands together. They sat there in silence, rejoicing about settling their differences. Oh, they would share many over the course of their lives, but Max no longer viewed the world through his terms of acceptance. Instead, he valued Vivian and her thoughts as a matter of importance. Also, he no longer cared about his pretentious status among his peers, especially after he had witnessed the disgrace of their character. Vivian and the children had taught him that happiness and love mattered above all else.

If Vivian accepted his atonement, for the rest of their lives, he would never give her doubt about his love. He would cherish the precious gift of her love close to his heart and spend every day making sure happiness surrounded them.

There were no words to describe how secure Max made her feel while she lay wrapped in his arms. She understood his reasons for breaking the betrothal. While it had caused her extreme heartache at the time, she believed it was for the best. Because if they had wed and Max hadn't believed in their love, then they would've suffered a disastrous union. She had floated through their previous courtship, a young maiden filled with innocence, not understanding how evil lurked under the pretense of her peers. Now she was a woman who understood the harsh realities of life but also recognized the goodness in those who mattered.

They still had much to overcome, but their love would see them through the darkness and into the fresh light of possibilities. She'd fallen in love with the idea of Max and not the man himself. Now, her heart was overfilled with the love she held for him. He made her dreams come true. He was her knight rescuing the damsel in distress. When she was at her lowest, he held out his hand for her to take.

Vivian looked at their fingers clasped together and smiled at the simple act that bonded them and the symbol of the gesture.

"Yes, I will marry you, my love."

Epilogue

False Rumors

*T*WO MONTHS LATER

Vivian waited outside, believing if she stared long enough, the carriage would arrive. Her sister was due to arrive any minute with Joy and her husband, Bradley. Max had persuaded her mother to allow Chloe to stay with them for the holidays. Vivian couldn't wait to share her new life with Chloe.

Max had wanted to whisk Vivian back to Scotland and marry her without the fuss. However, his mother had refused and convinced Max that Vivian deserved the wedding of her dreams and to show the ton how they rose above their slander. With much reluctance, he had posted the banns and waited the proper three weeks before they spoke their vows.

They still dealt with the upheaval of her family's problems. Max stood firm on never allowing them to hurt her again. And Vivian had yet to forgive them for turning her away. The only shining person was her sister, who she would never turn away.

They never discovered who wrote the letters to Vivian and her friends, and there had been no more threats issued. The ton whispered a fresh set of rumors, declaring Vivian and her friends were indeed governesses and they all held innocent virtues. Max continued his search for the culprit, but to no avail, the person remained a mystery.

The children were ecstatic that Vivian would never leave them again, and they flourished during their stay in London. However, they were all thrilled to return to Scotland.

The children played not far away with their friends. Vivian's friends and their employers, who Max had befriended, waited on the terrace for the guests to arrive. It was Max's idea to welcome Chloe with a friendly party.

Vivian smiled to herself at the simplicity of the life she had never imagined she would share with Max. Yet it was one they had settled into with a contentment that left one breathless from the sheer joy of its existence.

When Max wrapped his arms around her waist, Vivian jumped but settled back with a sigh. He held her against him and teased, "They will not appear magically because you watch for them, Lady Courtland."

She turned around in his arms. "Perhaps they will, Lord Courtland."

Max smirked, quirking an eyebrow. "Another hidden talent of yours?"

Vivian blushed, understanding the meaning behind his question. "Behave."

He chuckled at the rosiness of her cheeks. "Mmm." Max bent his head and suckled on her neck.

Vivian melted against him. "You must stop."

Max nipped a kiss on the corner of her lip, teasing a response. "Must I?"

He drew her lips under his, thirsty for a taste of her. It had been hours since he awakened with her underneath him, moaning his name. Also, he loved to fluster her until she succumbed to his charms.

Vivian groaned at how he teased her. He wasn't playing fair. "You are incorrigible. But 'tis what I love about you."

Max lifted his head, offering her a wicked smile. "And I love you, my dear. And I plan on showing you how incorrigible I can be later this evening once I have you all to myself."

His comment gave her pause. "Are you sure my sister is welcome to stay with us?"

Max brushed a stray curl from her face. "Yes, my love. She will be a joy to have. Plus, I plan to use her visit to my advantage."

Vivian chuckled. "How so?"

Max winked. "You shall see."

Before Vivian could question his mischievous answer, a carriage rumbled up the road. Once it stopped, Chloe flew out of the carriage and into Vivian's arms. They hugged each other, giggling with excitement.

Max smiled as he admired the exuberance of his wife. A few months ago, she had returned to his life full of bitterness, which he had caused. However, now she blossomed every day into a lady filled with happiness for those she loved.

Sometimes one must suffer through heartache to find eternal bliss.

Check out the next book in the False Rumors series in August/September 2023

"Thank you for reading The Fallen Governess. Gaining exposure as an independent author relies mostly on word-of-mouth, so if you have the time and inclination, please consider leaving a short review wherever you can."

Want to join my mailing list? Visit www.lauraabarnes.com today!

Desire other books to read by
Laura A. Barnes

Enjoy these other romances:

Historical Romances

False Rumors Series:
The Fallen Governess

Fate of the Worthingtons Series:

The Tempting Minx
The Seductive Temptress
The Fiery Vixen
The Siren's Gentleman

Matchmaking Madness Series:
How the Lady Charmed the Marquess
How the Earl Fell for His Countess
How the Rake Tempted the Lady
How the Scot Stole the Bride
How the Lady Seduced the Viscount
How the Lord Married His Lady

Tricking the Scoundrels Series:
Whom Shall I Kiss... An Earl, A Marquess, or A Duke?
Whom Shall I Marry... An Earl or A Duke?
I Shall Love the Earl
The Scoundrel's Wager
The Forgiven Scoundrel

Romancing the Spies Series:
Rescued By the Captain
Rescued By the Spy
Rescued By the Scot
Romancing the Spies Collection Box Set

Contemporary Romances

Mitchell Winery Series:
Seduced by Fate

About Author Laura A. Barnes

International bestselling author Laura A. Barnes fell in love with writing in the second grade. After her first creative writing assignment, she dreamt of becoming an author. Many years went by with Laura filling her head full of story ideas and some funny fish songs she wrote while fishing with her family. In 2017, she made her dreams a reality. With her debut novel Rescued By the Captain, she has set out on the path of a published author.

When not writing, Laura can be found devouring her favorite romance books. Laura is married to her own Prince Charming (who for some reason or another thinks the heroes in her books are about him) who she enjoys traveling with and binging shows on streaming services. You can usually find her spending time with her children and grandchildren. Besides her love of reading and writing, Laura loves to travel. With her passport stamped in England, Scotland, and Ireland; she hopes to add more countries to her list soon.

While Laura isn't very good on the social media front, she loves to hear from her readers. You can find her on the following platforms:

You can visit her at ***www.lauraabarnes.com*** to join her mailing list.

Website: https://www.lauraabarnes.com/

Amazon: https://amazon.com/author/lauraabarnes

Goodreads: https://www.goodreads.com/author/show/16332844.Laura_A_Barnes

Facebook: https://www.facebook.com/AuthorLauraA.Barnes/

Instagram: https://www.instagram.com/labarnesauthor/

Twitter: https://twitter.com/labarnesauthor

BookBub: https://www.bookbub.com/profile/laura-a-barnes

TikTok: https://www.tiktok.com/@labarnesauthor

Printed in Great Britain
by Amazon

21574210R00113